MEET THE FOUNDING MEMBERS
OF THE ZODIAC CLUB

ABBY MARTIN: A typical *Aries,* Abby brings the Zodiac Club together. She's always prepared to help others, but her headstrong Aries nature sometimes gets in her way. Will her wild and wonderful whims prevail?

MARA BENNETT: Feminine and charming, she personifies the *Libra* spirit. She appreciates harmony, but it is difficult for her to make a decision. How can she become more decisive?

J. L. RICHTER: Makes cool *Scorpio* a reality with her aloof and independent spirit. Like all Scorpios, she's sure of what she wants and determined to get it. But what is the cost?

ELIZABETH LEONARD: A true *Pisces,* she's a friend who's easily trusted, but her trust in others leaves her vulnerable to being hurt. She has dreams of her own and for every friend in the club. But who comes first?

CATHY ROSEN: Makes her *Leo* sign ring true with confidence and charisma, but her eagerness for praise often overshadows her accomplishments!

JESSICA HOLLY: The friendly, outgoing *Virgo* dreams of finding the right boy and wonders if she'll find a Prince Charming who will meet her expectations. Will her yearnings ever be fulfilled?

PENNY ROSS: A whiz at tennis, she's the perfect *Sagittarius*—zany but endearing! With her flare on the court and her fierce loyalty to her friends she's just not made for the ordinary, but will she make a superstar?

J.L. Richter

Mara Bennett

Elizabeth Leonard

Abby Martin

Jessica Holly

Cathy Rosen

Penny Ross

ARIES RISING

Including Famous People
Born under Each Sign

Sarah Godfrey

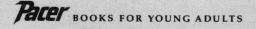 **BOOKS FOR YOUNG ADULTS**

a member of The Putnam Publishing Group
NEW YORK

Published by Pacer Books,
a member of the Putnam Publishing Group
51 Madison Avenue
New York, New York 10010

RL:6.2
Pacer is a trademark of The Putnam Publishing Group.
The Zodiac Club logo is a trademark of The Putnam
Publishing Group.

Printed in the United States of America
First printing

ARIES RISING

Compatibility and Love Chart

ARIES *(March 21—April 20)*

RULING PLANET: *Mars* SYMBOL: *The Ram*

★ ──────────────────────────────

Independence marks the Aries girl. Your ideal mate must accept you as a truly modern individual. You are passionate and brave, filled with ideals, and seek similar traits in your romantic partner. While you have a talent for accomplishing things quickly, be careful of hotheaded reactions when you should be more cautious. Both your boyfriends and girlfriends should be dynamic, involved, and able to keep up with your active interests and whimsical fantasies.

★ ──────────────────────────────

RELATIONSHIPS:

Aries & Aries—physical attraction, but often fireworks

Aries & Taurus—better for friendship than for romance

Aries & Gemini—romance possible, but keep your feet on the ground

Aries & Cancer—oversensitivity can cause difficulties

Aries & Leo—much excitement, challenges to be met

Aries & Virgo—stability, but a certain lack of passion

Aries & Libra—each needs the other

Aries & Scorpio—attraction, but much openness is needed

Aries & Sagittarius—fiery, energetic, a lot of fun

Aries & Capricorn—compromise is necessary

Aries & Aquarius—a surprising pair, good or bad

Aries & Pisces—challenging, potential for romance

"Abby, hurry up! We're going to be late for Levin's class," Mara Bennett called. "You know how ticked he gets if anyone's late. He'll keep us after, and I really don't want to miss the Zodiac Club meeting today." Mara rushed past Abby, clogs flapping. Abby's daydream was interrupted. She smiled and nodded.

Abby took a deep breath and sensed that special something in the air which announced spring had finally arrived. But Mara was right, she'd better hurry. Besides, botany was Abby's favorite class, Mr. Levin her favorite teacher. Abby turned and trotted after Mara, still thinking about how much she loved this time of year. It was, after all, the season of her birth, and she found it nearly miraculous that the earth seemed to be reborn during the same month she celebrated her own birthday. Abby was an Aries who believed her birth sign played an incredibly important part in her life.

The bell rang as they reached the door. Breathlessly, the two girls ducked into the room and slid into their seats.

Mr. Levin, tall, dark-haired, and handsome in a professorish sort of way, looked up from the papers he was sorting. "I'm glad to see that everybody made it today," he said. "I thought for a minute the two of you were going to play hooky." He glanced at Abby and smiled. "That would have been too bad, because I've got an announcement I know—or rather I hope—some of you will be interested in." Mr. Levin settled himself on the corner of the desk. "As you all undoubtedly know, two weeks from tomorrow, spring vacation begins."

Scattered cheers and clapping filled the room.

Mr. Levin continued. "Now, this is relatively late notice, but what I'd like to announce is that the science department in the person of yours truly is going to sponsor a four-day bike hike during vacation. We're going to the peak of Ram's Head Mountain to see the sun rise on the morning of the spring equinox. Along the way, we'll explore the botanical and geological specimens. The flora at this time of year is not bountiful, but it is really fascinating."

Mr. Levin paused. "I know we'll get a lot of exercise and hope we'll have the same amount of fun. The sign-up sheet is at the back of the room. There are places for twelve of you—so it's first come, first served. The cost is minimal, so I hope that some of you will want to come along. Now, back to serious work. Open your books to page two hundred, please."

During the rest of the period, Abby couldn't concentrate. She could picture herself standing at the peak of Ram's Head Mountain, watching the sun rise on the day of the equinox. She knew that the equinox, the first day of the sign Aries, had been special in ancient times, when spells and magic were woven closely into the fabric of everyday life. In her daydream she saw herself robed in white, her arms uplifted, a priestess of the dawn.

Abby had little planned for spring vacation, and she suddenly wanted nothing more than to go on this trip. It sounded so right that as soon as class was over, she went to the back of the room and signed at the top of the list.

"Gee, I wish I could go," Mara said as she looked over Abby's shoulder. "But my folks are taking me to my grandparents'. I love my gramps, but after awhile Altoona, Pennsylvania, gets just a *mite* boring. I hate to be away from Doug, too. Do you think that your folks will say it's okay to go? I know mine want me in Altoona."

"I don't know for sure," Abby answered, "but there are only twelve places and if I don't sign now, the trip might be closed by the time I talk it over with them."

Abby adjusted the books under her arm and started out the door. "Anyway," she said to Mara, "I'm sure they'll agree after I tell them about it."

"That's what I admire about you Aries people," Mara said as they walked toward their lockers. "You just forge ahead to get what you want. We poor Libras," she said with a sigh, "we spend several days analyzing the pros and cons before making up our minds."

"You didn't seem so analytic about asking Doug to the Winter Prom," Abby answered with a laugh.

"It seems that you were pretty decisive *that* time."

Mara blushed slightly, "Well, astrological signs don't govern every single thing people do and say, do they?"

"I don't know. We'll continue the discussion at the meeting. Wow, look at the time. Come on, they'll start without us. Everyone must have left for Elizabeth's house already."

When Mara and Abby finally arrived at the meeting, they were greeted by a querulous voice. "Well, at long last you decided to join us. I'm so glad you could pull yourself away from all your other pressing activities."

Abby shook her head slightly and looked at J.L. Richter, who lounged in a chair by the window. "Give it a rest, J.L., all right? We're only a couple of minutes late. You could have started without us. You knew we'd be here."

Abby and Mara settled themselves on the floor. The meeting began. Abby looked around the room. What a good group this was, she thought. She winked at her good friend Cathy Rosen, who sat in the corner.

Then there was Penny Ross, a typical Sagittarius if ever there was one. Penny was friendly, but she was *so* blunt. She lost a date only last week when she asked the starting guard on the basketball team if it was chocolate that made his face break out in all those red spots. Goodbye romance, before it even had a chance to get started.

Abby realized that all the members of the Zodiacs were special to her. I'm a lucky person, she thought to herself, to have so many friends.

Abby's thoughts were interrupted when Penny announced, "I've got an absolutely terrific thing for us to do. My folks just got back from Mexico, or else I would have said something sooner, but they've invited everyone who can make it to our lake house for the first weekend of vacation. I've convinced Dad to let a guy who works for him, who's really into astrology, come and do our charts professionally." Penny stopped and laughed brightly. "And I happen to know that our astrologer for the weekend is very, very cute!"

"And probably very married and very old," said Elizabeth Leonard.

"Why, thirty's not *that* old, is it?" Penny asked with a pout.

Everybody else groaned.

"Old or not," said Elizabeth, "it sounds like fun and I'd like to get out of my house. Count me in."

"Me too," said Jessica Holly, the club's perpetual partygoer. "I'll have to check with my folks, but it sounds great."

Abby felt a twinge. She didn't always like Penny's sarcastic attitude, but the weekend did sound like it had great possibilities. Why did it have to be at the same time as the bike trip? Maybe she could convince someone to join her on the trip to the mountain. No one else was an Aries, but someone still might be interested.

Abby finally spoke up, "I guess the weekend at the lake will be a lot of fun, Penny, but I can't come. Mr. Levin is sponsoring a four-day bike trip. It's to Ram's Head Mountain and I've signed up. I want to make the legend come true, especially since it applies to me, Aries the Ram. I was hoping that all of you would go, too."

"But Abby," said Elizabeth, "it'll be so cold up there I couldn't stand it. You know us Pisces— more comfortable on the beach than on top of a windy mountain."

None of the Zodiacs seemed interested in the bike trip. By the end of the meeting, Abby half wished she could bring herself to change her mind. But when she thought some more about it, she became convinced that she was going to see the sun rise on March twenty-first from the top of Ram's Head Mountain, and that was that.

Abby's resolve was tested again when she asked her parents for permission to go on the trip.

". . . Oh please, Dad," she said. "It's really going to be worthwhile."

"It's going to fall on the vernal equinox," said her father, looking over his glasses. "You know that your mother and I are not thrilled by your obsession with astrology. Don't try to tell me that the reason for your wanting to go on this field trip doesn't have something to do with that."

Abby signed. Her father always had been able to read her like a book. There would be no use in trying to be evasive.

"Well . . ." Abby hesitated, then gave the smile her father called "the bomb" because it blew away all his objections. The smile often worked and Abby knew that although her father loved her deeply, he sometimes didn't understand why certain things were so important.

"You're right, Dad, to a degree. The fact that I'll

be on top of Ram's Head on the morning of March twenty-first does mean something to me, but astrology is just one of my interests. I'm not obsessed! Don't make it sound like black magic. It's *not*. You know that. I like botany and geology, and you know what a good teacher Mr. Levin is. After all, you're the one who's always grumbling that the school doesn't offer enough enrichment. And besides, I really don't have much to do over spring vacation . . ."

"She's right," her mother added. "Being out of doors will be good for Abby."

"Well," her father answered, "we'll see."

That was good enough for Abby. A "we'll see" turned into a "yes" ninety-nine times out of a hundred.

The next day, when Abby read the list of names of those who had signed up to go on the trip, she began to wish that her father had been firmer in his objections. There wasn't a single person listed whom she considered a friend—and those she did know a little—well, she'd never really felt a desire to be friends with them.

There was Mitchell Gavin, boy scientist. How, she wondered, would he find time to break away from his beloved experiments long enough to go riding in the country? From all that she could tell, he seemed like one of the class nerds. There was nothing wrong with brains, but he was just so serious. It wasn't that Mitchell was bad-looking or anything, but he seemed too bookish and immersed in his work for Abby's taste. He certainly wasn't for her, but maybe someone in the Zodiac Club would be right for him. Maybe Jessica.

And if Mitchell wasn't bad enough, Tracey
Kingsport had signed up, too. She must have been
in Mr. Levin's other class. What was it that Mara
called Tracey? Sour tongue? No. Viper, that was it!
And Abby had to agree. If there were a possibility
of puncturing anyone's balloon, Tracey was always
ready with the verbal pins. Abby had taken a history
class with her last year, and they hadn't agreed on
a single issue. When Abby said it was tragic that
the French revolution turned into a bloodbath with
the revolutionaries turning on each other, Tracey
sighed in a bored way and made some crack about
sentimentality having no place in a political revolution.

Then she dramatically added her own philosophy,
"We're all just like fish in the sea. Eventually, the
big fish eat the little fish. It's all about power and
greed of one sort or another, isn't it?"

Abby refused to see life that way. There were
causes worth fighting for and believing in. There
just had to be. Unfortunately, it looked as though
she was going to be stuck with Tracey for four days!

Abby continued to scan the sign-up sheet. She
didn't recognize any of the other names until she
got to Bill Kelsey. There was someone who might
be fun. Abby had seen him around school. Everyone
said he was a hell-raiser but thought he had a great
sense of humor. He really was attractive, having the
rugged good looks Abby couldn't help noticing. But
like Mitchell, Abby wasn't so sure Bill was her type
either, and besides there was Buddy to think about.

Besides, one Kelsey didn't make a successful trip.

Abby was just about to take her pen and cross out her name when she heard a familiar voice in back of her.

"That certainly looks like a great group for you to spend most of spring vacation with——a bunch of lost campers!"

Abby turned around to see Penny Ross. "Or," Penny continued, "perhaps I should say losers. Too bad. We're going to have so much fun at my house. Come on, Abby, change your mind and come. Please? Oh, I forgot. Once Abby Martin makes up her mind to do something, only a major crisis, like the end of the world, will make her change it."

Abby tried not to show Penny that she was getting angry. Why didn't Penny ever think about anyone but herself? Didn't it occur to her that she could hurt other people's feelings?

Abby managed a slight smile. "Penny, I don't know how you can say that. Why are you so close-minded? I was just thinking it was high time I expanded my horizons and socialized with some of the other people in this high school. I know that you guys will have fun. But for me, *another* overnight with the *same* familiar faces, it seems just a bit . . . well, you know, *boring.* Got to go now."

Before Penny had a chance to answer, Abby turned and walked away. She would go on this bike trip. She would meet new people, she would learn new things and, darn it, she was going to have fun—— even if it killed her.

_____ 2 ★

"You're Abby Martin, aren't you?" the voice next
to her asked. "You don't know me, but I'm Marilyn
Brownlow. I saw that you signed up for the bike
trip. Me too. I'm in Levin's other class. I hope it'll
be good."

Abby looked at Marilyn. Of course she knew her.
Everybody at school knew Marilyn. Only a sophomore, she was a varsity field hockey player and sophomore class vice president. She was also good-looking
in the corn-fed, blond, all-American way that boys
found so appealing. She had, Abby thought, probably been good-looking since she was born. Marilyn
was the kind of girl that teachers remembered for
years after she graduated.

Abby nodded. "Hi! Glad to meet you. Going to
the meeting Mr. Levin's called?"

Marilyn smiled, and Abby couldn't help but notice her perfect teeth. Was there anything wrong
with this person? she thought and then immediately
regretted the pettiness of her reaction. Marilyn
seemed to radiate the quality "nice."

"Yes, I am," Marilyn answered. "I have to say

_16_

I'm a little nervous about the trip. I really don't know anyone who's going, but Mr. Levin's really terrific, and I couldn't stand the thought of hanging around for the vacation. Do you think it will be okay?"

Abby suddenly felt like an older, protective sister. "Of course it will," she answered. "We'll have fun and learn something too. Who knows? Maybe we'll all come back best friends."

When they entered the classroom where the meeting was to be held, they heard a high-pitched giggle pierce the air. Marilyn wrinkled her nose and whispered, "That doesn't sound like best-friend material to me. Does it to you?"

Abby laughed. Marilyn had a sense of humor. Good. She'd be someone to talk to on the trip.

The minute hand on the big wall clock made its loud ticking noise and, as if on cue, Mr. Levin entered.

"I'm glad almost all of you could make it. There will be nine of us. Mr. Kelsey isn't here I see, but let's get started. I think it's important that we introduce ourselves and get to know each other a bit before we take off on this springtime adventure."

Heads around the room nodded in agreement. Mr. Levin continued, "I know you all probably have other important things to do—such as homework." He paused as groans filled the room. "We'll all get to know each other better on the trip, but for now I think it would be useful to tell the others why you're going on the trip and what you hope to get out of it. Okay? Now, who'd like to be first?"

Abby glanced around the room. She could see that no one in this group of relative strangers wanted to go first.

Mr. Levin waited for a few seconds, then shook his head. "Well," he said, "I hope it's not going to be this quiet on the trip. If it is, I, for one, am not going to have any fun. All right," he added, "to break the ice, the old teacher will go first. As you know, I'm Mr. Levin. I've taught all of you. I've organized this trip because I like the countryside; I like the exercise; and, contrary to rumor, I really do like high-school young people. If it doesn't sound too corny, let me add that I like to see kids discovering interesting things about their environment and themselves. And for all those who are curious, my wife gets no vacation at this time of year, so the trip is my personal vacation and nature outing." Amid the laughter that followed, Mr. Levin said, "All right, who's next?" His eyes scanned the room.

From a seat several rows behind Abby came the giggle again. "I'll go next, Mr. Levin. My name is Fannie Green and I'm a freshman, but you know that because you said I could come because I'm really interested in botany." Another giggle.

That giggle is going to drive me crazy, Abby thought to herself.

"And all my friends were going away for vacation," Fannie continued, "so I thought that this might be a terrific way to spend the week."

Marilyn sighed and rolled her eyes at Abby.

Oh, well, I guess if I were a freshman named Fannie Green I'd giggle nervously, too, Abby thought, but I hope she'll improve once she gets to know everyone.

"Great, Fannie," said Mr. Levin. "Fannie is an excellent science student when she wants to be. How about you, Ms. Martin?" he said, looking at Abby.

Abby was never shy about speaking up in public, and since she had been called on, she began, "My name is Abby Martin. I'm a junior. I'm going on this trip for a couple of reasons. First, I think I'll learn something about nature, but second, I'm an Aries, and . . ."

A snort came from the back of the room. Abby looked around and saw Tracey grimacing and slowly shaking her head as if in disbelief.

"*And,*" Abby said with more purpose in her voice, "the day we're supposed to arrive at Ram's Head is the first day of my sign. It may sound overly romantic and some of you may find this amusing, but there's an old legend about the mountain and I'd love to be there on the day the sun rises."

"Well, Abby," Mr. Levin said, "I prefer your interest in science, but you have some interesting motivation. You'll have to tell us the legend some time."

Tracey ran her fingers through her hair and said, "I'll go next. My name is Tracey Kingsport, and I'm not interested in superstitious twaddle." Fannie started to giggle, but she stopped right away when Tracey turned and glared at her. "As a senior who has a college boyfriend who won't be free on my spring break, I decided to sign up for the trip on this, my last spring vacation, of high school. I like cycling and," she added coolly, "I like Mr. Levin. However, had I known that I'd be traveling with someone who does an imitation of a hyena, plus a zodiac freak, I . . ."

"I think that's unnecessary, Tracey," Mr. Levin interrupted.

Before he could go any further, the door of the classroom opened and Bill Kelsey strolled in.

"'Afternoon, folks," he said, his eyes twinkling. "Sorry I'm late. I couldn't get away from my earlier appointment. Kelsey provides good times all the time."

Suddenly, with the entrance of this dark-haired, muscular young man, Abby could sense a change in the atmosphere of the room.

"Yes, you can do something for us," said Mr. Levin, who was obviously not amused by Bill Kelsey. "You can be on time in the future. But now we are introducing ourselves to each other and telling why we are going on the trip. Since you've decided to honor us with your presence, why don't you go next?"

"No sweat," Bill answered. "I'm going on the trip to have fun. I *always* have fun, 'cause if there's no fun, I make some."

Mr. Levin's eyes narrowed slightly. "Well, Bill," he said, "I'd hoped you'd care a bit about the science part of this. Let's hope you'll find all the fun you want on the trip as planned. We've got much to explore, so you won't have to use too much ingenuity thinking up ways to keep yourself amused."

"Right, Mr. Levin. Whatever you say," Bill replied as he slid into a desk. "Whatever you say."

He looked at Mr. Levin directly, cocked his head, and gave the teacher a small, confident grin.

"Next," Mr. Levin called. There was a shifting sound from the back of the room and the overweight boy, who was sandwiched into a desk, began to talk. "I guess I might as well go next. I can't put it off forever. My name is Dale Chambers. I'm a sophomore, and I'm going on this trip as a bribe to my parents. Don't get me wrong, I love science and it will probably be lots of fun—if I don't have to pedal a hundred miles a day."

"Don't worry about that," Mr. Levin said. "I'm not quite such a taskmaster."

"I'm glad to hear it," Dale said in a resigned voice, "but I bet my parents wouldn't be. They want me to toughen myself up and," he paused and added quietly, "lose a little weight. They gave me the choice of gradually taking the pounds off or of going to one of those camps for fatties this summer. I mean I'm *not* going to go to one of those places, no way, so I thought that I could show them that I was really trying by signing up for this trip."

"What do they think of the idea?" Mr. Levin asked.

"They think it's terrific," Dale answered. Then he pitched his voice high in an imitation of his mother and said, "'Oh, Dale, you're such a handsome boy, if you will only give yourself the chance. I know this trip will be *such* fun, and you'll come back well on the way to being my own handsome movie star.' When she says that stuff, I want to run into the kitchen and eat another dozen Twinkies."

Everyone in the classroom laughed, but Abby

thought that whether or not Dale had movie-star potential, his mother was right. He could stand to lose twenty pounds.

"Well, I'm not going on the trip to shape up or just to have fun," said the boy in the front of the room. Abby knew him. He was Tom Watkins. He often was at the edge of the crowd at the parties she went to, but he never seemed to enter into the center of things. He dressed like a preppie and once at one of the meetings of the Zodiac Club when his name had been mentioned, J.L. had said he had potential but was uptight. He had, J.L. reported, his whole life planned out. He was going to try to get into a big-name college, then go on to get a graduate degree in business and make a lot of money. Elizabeth added that he sounded like someone to avoid like the plague and Abby couldn't help agreeing with her.

"I'm going on this bike trip to do myself some good." Tom continued, "I'm a junior, and I'm going on this trip because my folks and I think it will look good on my college application. It will show a serious interest in science and be an interesting topic for my essay."

"Oh, come off it," Tracey muttered.

"No, it's true," Tom continued, "and I'm not ashamed to admit it. I mean, after all, what's high school about except getting into the right college, so you can get into the right grad school, right?"

"He's got to be kidding!" Marilyn groaned.

"I'm not," he said. "I figure that this trip will make me look like an off-beat, interesting kind of guy. You know, another aspect of my personality."

"And are you an off-beat kind of guy?" Mitchell asked, trying to conceal his amusement.

"No, I don't really think so," Tom said with a shrug.

"You certainly win points for candor," Mr. Levin said. "I hope you also like science."

"If it doesn't look good on his activity sheet, no way," Tracey said.

Mr. Levin, sensing that the conversation was going off in the wrong direction again, turned and said, "Now, how about you, Mitchell? We've heard from the other boys. Why are you coming on the trip?"

Abby glanced across the room to where Mitchell sat. Sure enough, his desk was piled high with textbooks and topped with a calculator in a black pouch. Her first impression of him, Abby concluded, was probably correct; the complete computer nut.

Mitchell at up in his seat and looked around the room, taking in the other students who were there. Then he turned back to Mr. Levin.

"I like botany, astronomy, and every science, so I signed up. I never thought about other reasons. But now this trip looks like it may turn out like one of those World War Two movies — you know, the kind — *Fighting Yanks*. The movie brings together ten guys — all of them different in background and attitude, but they're all out on a mission to save the world. It seems like this group is all different. We're definitely not going to save the world, but I bet something interesting will come from the trip. Maybe we can call ourselves 'High-

Schoolers on the Highway,' and someone will make a movie about us. Oh, yes, I forgot, I'm Mitchell Gavin, and I'm a junior, too."

Abby smiled. Mitchell's enthusiasm had made her feel good, and she wondered what his sign was. I'll bet he's a Cancer—calm, directed, in control, she thought. She started to think of the trip as a way to get to know eight other people.

Tracey might turn out to be bearable or funny under that sour exterior. What if Marilyn wasn't as self-confident as she looked? Probably Dale was just as wimpy as he looked, but maybe someone could get Fannie to stop giggling. And there was Bill Kelsey, Abby thought. He seemed so relaxed and cool. She was sure he would be fun even if most of the others weren't. Those twinkling eyes of his might be just what the trip needs, Abby told herself. As for Mitchell Gavin . . .

"Okay. That does it," Mr. Levin said. Abby realized that she had been lost in her thoughts right through Marilyn's comments.

Darn, Abby thought. Oh, well, I'll have to find out about Marilyn while we're on the trip. I'm sure we'll talk.

"Saturday morning we'll meet at the supermarket off Main Street," Mr. Levin said. "We'll do the shopping for the trip. Each of you remember to bring fifteen dollars. We'll divide the provisions and everyone will have his or her responsibility. Here's a list of gear you'll need."

As they left the room, Marilyn turned to Abby. "Things got a bit touchy in there, didn't they?" she said.

"But I think it's going to be all right," Abby answered. "Some people have something to say about everything. It will work out. At least everybody was pretty honest about their reasons."

"I sure hope so," said Marilyn. "I wouldn't want to live through four days of squabbling. Got to go to practice now. See you Saturday."

"Okay," Abby answered and watched as Marilyn moved away from her and down the hall. Abby counted four male heads that turned to stare at Marilyn. Lucky girl, Abby thought.

"Well, how did it go?" asked Mara Bennett, approaching from behind Abby. "I see that you have made the acquaintance of Collingwood's most popular sophomore."

"Who, Marilyn? She seems nice," answered Abby. "She's just pretty, popular, and talented, but that doesn't make her all bad, does it?"

"You're right. Doug's sister sits next to her in English, and she says that Marilyn's terrific. If Janie, Ms. Envy-of-the-Year, can say that about someone as pretty as Marilyn, she must be all right. How were the others?"

"Well, let's just say it's a mixed bag. Some of them are pretty weird. Bill Kelsey looks as if he'll be fun though."

"Bill Kelsey? Isn't he the one who hung around with that bunch of wild seniors last year? I'm not sure, but I think I heard that he had something to do with Tony Blake getting expelled."

"Tony Blake?"

"You remember, that kid who 'borrowed' Mrs. Loomis's car, and returned it all banged up and full of flour. Doug told me about it. When Mrs. Loomis came out of the building and saw her poor dented car, she ran to it like a maniac, yanked open the door, and white powder sort of exploded out of it. The poor lady turned into the Pillsbury Dough Teacher in a matter of seconds. Doug was in the lot when it happened, and I know it sounds terrible to say, but he said it *was* awfully funny. I guess she didn't think so, though, because within the week she had found out who had done it, and Tony Blake was O-U-T—out of school."

"But why did he do it?" Abby asked. "And what does that have to do with Bill Kelsey?"

"I'm not sure," Mara answered, "but I think Mrs. Loomis had flunked Tony's girlfriend in gym."

"Flunk gym?" Abby laughed. "Nobody flunks gym!"

"Listen, Abby, this girl was not known for her brilliance," Mara answered. "As for Kelsey, well, no one ever proved anything, but after it was all over, a couple of kids said they thought they saw him driving the car toward that overgrown place down by the town dump. He was trying to impress the seniors."

"Kelsey doesn't strike me as the kind who would get involved with a vindictive jerk," Abby answered.

"Hey, what do I know?" Mara answered. "I'm just telling you what I heard. Listen, if he's the only one in the group who looks promising, why don't you forget it? You can still go to Penny's. She'll lord it over you for a while because you changed your mind, but so what? It might be fun."

Abby had to admit she was tempted by Mara's

suggestion, but her Aries independence was strong, and she shook her head. "Thanks, Mara. You might be right, but I'd feel as if I were letting down Mr. Levin, and I really do want to take the trip. If all the others turn out to be losers, I'll just bike along in solitary splendor and make the best of it. Maybe I'm too hard on them. First impressions and all that. Do you know anything about Mitchell Gavin? I thought he was a science nut, period, but he actually seemed all right. He's not exactly an Adonis, but his comments were good."

Abby and Mara strolled the nearly empty after-school halls.

"I guess you wouldn't know about Mitchell since you went to the other elementary school. He and J.L. were a puppy love item when we were all back in sixth grade! He was always nice, kind of serious. He will definitely not be voted best-looking boy in our class, but he's not bad. Of course, he's not Doug or Buddy." Mara smiled.

The two girls emerged from the school and faced a sky suddenly obscured by leaden clouds. An icy breeze reminded them that winter hadn't completely disappeared, and Mara shivered. "Brrr, I'm freezing. Got to run. Abby, are you *sure* you won't change your mind about the trip? I bet they can get someone to take your place. Everyone wants you at Penny's."

Abby smiled. "No thanks. You're sweet to ask again. They'll have fun at Penny's. You'll have fun at your grandfather's and I'll have a good time on my trip. I'll call you as soon as I get home and we can compare notes."

"Whatever you say. You have the right idea. We'll

both manage." Mara hunched her shoulders and trotted off into the wind.

Abby watched her for a minute, then turned and began to walk home. She had a mountain of homework to do. I can hardly wait for vacation to begin, Abby thought. I'll even have a day to sleep late before I go off on the trip.

"Abby," she said out loud, "list as many good things as possible that may happen on this vacation. Then you'll feel better about it. One, you'll get to see the sun rise on the day of the vernal equinox. Two, Mr. Levin is a great and interesting teacher. You will learn some fascinating things. Three, you'll get needed exercise. Four, Bill Kelsey looks handsome and fun, and Mitchell Gavin might not be as bad as your first impression. Five, . . ." but as Abby thought, she really couldn't come up with a fifth good thing. Well, she had a week to find number five.

3

During the next few days Abby readied her ten-speed bike for the trip. She brought out her helmet from a duffel bag in the basement. She hated wearing it because it was hot and it really messed up her hair, but she knew the rules. Mr. Levin would never allow anyone on the roads without a helmet. In fact, the rule was a good one, Abby had to admit. Even around town, there were times when speeding cars or junk in the roadway made her nervous about falling. Imagine what a highway would be like, even a highway that was only two lanes. No, the helmet was a pain, but it was necessary.

Three o'clock Friday afternoon finally arrived and spring vacation officially began. Everyone congregated at the diner after school, but the conversation was dominated by Penny, who repeated the plans for her party. Abby couldn't join in the spirit and quietly left early.

"Speak to you before I head out," she called to everyone as she left.

The telephone was ringing as she entered her house. "I'll get it, Mother," Abby called as she dropped her books and grabbed the phone.

"Buddy," Abby announced with surprise when she heard the voice at the other end. "I can't believe it's you. This is great."

Abby was surprised to hear Buddy Randall. She'd met him through her friend J.L. at the end of the summer. He was off at college and although he hardly ever wrote, they had seen each other over vacation. That didn't mean, of course, he didn't like her. Most boys never wrote letters. But still, she sometimes thought that if Buddy really liked her, he could send her a postcard. Now, all her doubts faded as she heard his voice.

"Abby, I know that this is last-minute, but my friend's brother Jeff Symms from Collingwood is driving up here tomorrow morning. I hoped you'd hitch a ride with him and visit me for the weekend. You know I've been trying to figure out how to get you up here."

"Oh, Buddy, I don't believe this. I'd love to. I miss you, but I'm supposed to leave first thing tomorrow morning on a four-day bike trip with my botany teacher and a group of kids from school."

"Can't you cancel?" Buddy asked. "Really, Abby, it would be great to see you."

"It's so tempting. But I can't, Buddy. You don't know what I've been going through. I was just going to write you all about it. You see, I was tempted to back out of this bike trip because this weekend Penny is having a party for the Zodiacs at her lake house. I mean, I made a decision to do something different, on my own, and I have to go through with it."

"Well, it sounds like more of a chore than a good time." Buddy replied. "But if you don't want to come . . ."

"Oh, Buddy, please don't make it hard. Of course I want to see you, but a decision is a decision. After all, you *are* asking me at the last minute." Abby bit her lip as she waited for him to answer. She didn't know why she was starting a fight with him. She wanted to see Buddy, but her Aries stubbornness said she had to go on the bike trip.

"Okay, Abby, you win. I just wish you had been free. Maybe you can get up here for house parties next month—if you can fit it into your busy schedule."

"I'd love to, Buddy," Abby replied.

"Well, I'll call you again and we'll see," he said sarcastically.

"Oh, Buddy, don't be mad," Abby said.

"I'm not." Buddy answered. "Really, have fun. Take care. Bye." And he hung up.

Abby put the phone down and sighed. What had she done now?

When the alarm rang at eight on Saturday morning, she didn't feel in the least bit sleepy. The morning sky held the promise of a gorgeous day to come. As Abby padded down the hall to the shower, she was determined to feel good about striking off on the road. Today the group would shop, and tomorrow they would be off. She decided not to think one bit about Buddy, and she dressed quickly. Going downstairs, she decided to send him a card from the road. She wanted to go to house parties. She hoped the invitation would still be open when she came home. Abby gave her mother a big smile when she looked up from the paper she was reading at the breakfast table.

"'Morning, Mom. Looks like it's going to be a great day, doesn't it?"

"Good morning, Abby. You sound in a good mood. You must be looking forward to the trip if you're up so early on your first day of vacation."

"I really am. I'm determined to have a super time."

"I don't want to be the voice of gloom," her father began, "but the extended forecast isn't great. They say there's a sixty percent chance of rain moving in during the next couple of days. Do you have a poncho or something?"

"Don't worry, Dad. I've got it all. Mr. Levin supplied us with a list of the basics, so I'm all set. But it's not going to rain." Abby held her spoon like a scepter. "I won't allow it to. The power of my positive thinking will send all rain to Florida to surprise all those beach bums who are planning to come back to school and show off their tans. Me, I'll be burnished bright by warm sun and gentle breezes."

"You're positively poetic today," her mother answered, smiling. "I'm glad you're looking forward to it. Just be careful out there on the road."

"Of course. Mr. Levin will be there, and nothing's going to happen. Listen, can I have the car for an hour or so? We're going on a supplies safari, and I may have to haul some stuff to other kids' houses as well as bring what I'm going to pack back here."

"Sure," her mother answered.

"Thanks. See you later."

Abby banged out the back door and jumped down the stairs leading to the backyard. Her eye caught a bright spot of color on the side of the path leading to the garage. She laughed with delight as she saw, standing brave and true, the first crocuses of the season. This was definitely a good omen for the trip, Abby thought. She hopped into the car and backed down the driveway. She was off for a great day.

When she reached the parking lot, she saw that most of the other kids who were going on the trip were already clustered around Mr. Levin.

Abby parked the car and walked toward the group. Most of them had their eyes closed, their faces turned to the sky in an attempt to drink in the warmth of the bright spring sun.

"You guys look just like the crocuses I just saw in my driveway. All those bright faces turned upward."

"Hi, Abby," Mr. Levin said. "Only Fannie and Bill are missing now. We'll give them a couple of minutes. Come and join the sun worshipers."

"Thanks, I will. Hi, Marilyn. Can I squeeze into the pack?"

"Sure, Abby," Marilyn answered cheerfully.

Tracey turned her head slightly and, keeping her eyes shut, said in an icy voice, "Really, Marilyn. Must you be so bright and cheerful this early in the morning."

Marilyn looked at her with surprise. "Sorry I offended you," she responded sarcastically.

Tracey didn't let it go.

"I can't handle idle chatter before eleven A.M., especially when it's Miss Goody-Two-Shoes being greeted by Little Mary Sunshine," Tracey continued.

All the closed eyes suddenly popped open at Tracey's remarks.

"What did you have for breakfast, acid?" Tom quipped.

Abby's cheeks turned bright red as she remembered her past experience with Tracey.

"What's the matter?" Tracey whined, as she saw Abby's face. "Doesn't the queen of the Zodiac Club take criticism well? Isn't she a perfect Aries?"

"Abby may be queen of the Zodiacs, but you, Tracey, seem to be chief witch. Or do I have the first letter wrong?" Mitchell joined in.

The conversation was interrupted by the slam of a car door and a high-pitched giggle. "Sorry everyone, my alarm didn't go off, or I just slept through it," Fannie declared as she joined the group with her usual grin on her face.

"It's all right, Fannie," Mr. Levin said. "The rest of us just arrived." He checked his watch. "But we are running slightly behind, so I think we had better get started. Mr. Kelsey, if he decides to show up, can join us inside. This is the last time we'll wait. His rations might be on the short side by the time the trip is over." He paused, frowned slightly, and then continued. "Okay. Here's what we're going to do. We don't want to load ourselves down more than we have to, so you'll see that I haven't included many canned goods on the list. While we'll be eating nutritionally, we won't be stuffing ourselves."

"Great," said Dale Chambers ironically. "I'll come

back a lean, mean, cycling machine."

Tracey whispered to Tom, "Good luck to lard-butt."

Mr. Levin, obviously not hearing her remark, continued, "I can't make any promises, Dale, but it wouldn't surprise me if you did drop a few pounds on the trip and come back feeling good. Now, for the supplies. In the interest of time, and so we won't clog the aisles, I've made up two lists. I've assigned each of you to one of two groups. Each group will buy the things on its list. Simple, yes? Carefully substitute if you can't find what's listed. But remember the budget is limited."

Everyone nodded. "Fine," Mr. Levin continued. "Here are the lists with the names. Tracey, you head up one team, and . . ."

Abby took a step forward, sure somehow that she would be asked to take charge of the other team, but Mr. Levin didn't look at her. "Tom, you be in charge of the other group," he said.

Abby felt herself color. She was sure that no one else had noticed her assumption, but she still felt slightly embarrassed. It was just that she was good at organizing, and most people recognized that quality in her and were glad to let her do it.

"It's no big deal," she said to herself, realizing that if any members of the Zodiac Club had been with her she would have confessed her gaff, and laughed. "Aries are always convinced they can do the job better than anyone else." She could almost hear J.L.'s words.

"Come on, Abby," Tom interrupted her thoughts, "you're with me. So are you, Fannie, and so is Kelsey if he ever shows up. Our list is about twenty items. Let's go."

The two groups entered the supermarket. Ever since she had been a little girl, Abby had a sense of amazement when she went into a supermarket. When she was small, she wondered how food grown all over the world ended up in her neighborhood store. It seemed miraculous. She once asked her mother if Santa Claus helped deliver the groceries to each store. Her question had long since become a standing joke in the family.

"Hi, Abby, you're up early for the first day of vacation."

Abby interrupted her reverie and turned to the voice. There, dressed in a light brown shirt with the name of the store stitched on the pocket was Dawn Simpson, a girl Abby had known in first grade. At one point in their grade-school years, she and Dawn had been friendly, playing on the swings and occasionally spending the night at each other's house. When they reached junior high school, each of them had developed other friends. They occasionally talked to each other in the halls, but they had gone their separate ways.

"Hi, Dawn," Abby answered. "You're up early, too. Got to work?"

"Yeah, Mr. Grey, the store manager, has to take his kid to the orthodontist, and the assistant manager is sick. Mr. Grey asked me if I'd take over for a couple of hours this morning. It's sort of an honor to be asked. It's not a humungous big deal, but they don't give high-school kids much responsibility usually. Mr. Grey trusts me, though, and I think he's going to give me a fairly big raise in the next couple of weeks. If I stay on and work full time during vacations and next summer, the raise could make a big difference in my college plans. The money's been a bit tight around my house since my dad lost his job last year."

"Oh, I'm sorry, Dawn. I didn't know."

"That's okay. Anyway, he's back at work now in an even better job, but we had six tense months last summer and fall. We had to use savings and blah-blah-blah, so my college piggy bank isn't exactly bursting."

"Well," said Abby, "I think it's terrific that the manager thinks so much of you."

Dawn smiled. "I feel like a real businesswoman or something. Anyway, got to run and make sure everything is going smoothly."

"Sure. Take it easy. I'll see you."

"No pinching the melons, now," Dawn said as she left, "or I'll have to speak to you severely."

Abby laughed. "Don't worry. We'll be good."

Tom sighed impatiently. "Enough gab, Abby. Let's get going."

"Right," said Abby as she turned back to the other kids. "Let's get to it. Fannie, you get the basket. What's first on the list, Tom?"

He held out the piece of paper to her and she saw that among the fist things listed were dried soup, paper plates, and cheese.

"Let's get the soup first. Follow me," Abby said.

"Wait a minute," Tom answered. "Soup is all the way over on the other side of the store. Why not start with the plates? They're right in the aisle in front of us. At least that's what the sign says."

Abby couldn't help feeling a bit impatient. "Because," she said, "I think the best way to shop is to start at the place that is farthest away from the cash register, and then work your way back, so that when you're finished, you don't have to trundle all the way back across the store to pay. That makes sense, doesn't it?"

"Yeah, I guess it does," Fannie said. "But I always take a look at the list and buy the noncrushable items first. That way they're on the bottom, and," she giggled, "the fragile things like eggs and stuff don't get all smashed up."

"Well," Tom said, "it looks like we all have different strategies. I guess there's more than one way to fill a cart? However, since Mr. Levin asked me to head up this expedition, and even though I see nothing crushable on our list, Fan, I vote that we start with the aisle in front of us. We'll just have to spend the extra time and energy pushing the cart back across the store when we're through. Okay, Abby?"

"Whatever, you say, intrepid leader," Abby answered. She smiled. "It doesn't really matter how we fill up the cart in the great scheme of things, does it?"

Abby thought to herself that it really did matter how this shopping expedition was run. She wasn't the leader here. However, when they got to the paper plates, Abby started taking the cheapest, "no name" plates off the shelf, and she was surprised to hear Tom ask, "What are you doing?"

"Getting the plates. Isn't that what we're supposed to be getting?" Abby answered.

"But why those?"

"Because they are the cheapest, and Mr. Levin said that we have only so much money to spend," Abby answered. She was surprised to hear the slight note of annoyance that had crept into her voice. Her decision was the obvious one, wasn't it?

"Sorry, Abby," Tom said, "these may cost a bit more, but they're made of better paper, and they don't leak through. Ever tried to eat stew off a cheap paper plate? Before you know it, the gravy has leaked through and is all over your lap."

"Yeech," Fannie said.

"Yeech is right," Tom continued, "so if you buy the cheap ones, you wind up using two at a time, and in the long run it's not cheaper at all." He removed the plates Abby had put in the cart and substituted the ones he had chosen.

Abby had to admit that his argument was logical, but she also had to admit that she didn't like to be overruled. "Take it easy, Aries," she said to herself with a wary smile. "You may be a take-charge kind of person, but better go slow here."

"Well, look who's here," Tom said, "the last American soldier. We're almost through, Kelsey. Why don't you get the last item and meet us at the register. At least you can help load stuff into the cars. By that time, you might even be awake."

Bill did look as though he hadn't fully awakened yet, Abby thought. His eyes looked puffy and his hair was messy.

Bill yawned and said, "Why don't you cool it, Tom. We're not in business school now, you know. I was wrecked last night, so you can just write up my late arrival to the kind of off-beat behavior you think the college of your choice will be so interested in. Only please, don't yammer at me. You make my head feel worse."

"Oh? What bash were you at?" Fannie asked and then giggled nervously.

"Oh, one I'm not going to tell you about, my little laughing brook. I don't want to fill your dear little young head with tales of corruption and debauchery," Bill answered in his best W. C. Fields voice.

Fannie looked totally confused. Bill then turned toward Abby. "Good morning. You're looking fresh and lovely. Almost makes it worth getting out of the sack."

"'Morning, Bill," Abby answered. "I'm glad I wasn't at the same party as you. It looks like not many lived to tell the tale."

"All right," Tom said a bit peevishly, "now can we please get on with this? I really don't want to spend all morning in the supermarket."

"Go ahead, Tom. Come on, Abby, help me find this," Bill said.

"We'll meet up with Mr. Levin at the cash register. He has all the money," Tom called, and he and Fannie headed down the aisle.

"So tell me," Bill asked, "did you guys have a really intense time discussing whether it's better to get tuna packed in water or in oil, and which cookies do you really prefer, Miss Martin?" he asked, holding an imaginary microphone in front of Abby.

She walked along and laughed. "I thought you were supposed to be out of it," she said. "You obviously have enough energy to be a radio host."

"I've always got time for what I want to do." He grabbed an empty cart that was in an aisle and gave Abby a conspiratorial wink. "Hop on."

"Don't be ridiculous." Abby laughed. "I'm too big to sit in that thing."

"Not in the little seat," he laughed. "Get on top and let your gorgeous legs hang down. I'll give you a quickie free ride. Don't be chicken. Are you afraid to live dangerously?"

"Come on, Bill, stop being silly." Abby laughed again.

"Abby Martin, Aries *extraordinaire*, afraid of a little ride in a supermarket cart? I'll take you up aisle ten so you can see every soup can close up! Don't deny me this pleasure, Abby." Bill smiled and looked sincere.

"Oh, okay," Abby agreed, shaking her head as if giving in to a little boy's unreasonable but adorable demand.

She hopped on the cart and let her legs dangle over the side. Bill began pushing the cart slowly, then added speed until they were whizzing past soups, ketchup, mayonnaise, and pickles.

"Hey Bill, this is too fast for me," she said as she jumped off the cart, but Bill continued pushing. Abby started to yell, "Wait!" but the words seemed to stick in her throat. She watched in horror as the cart went careening around the corner and collided with a towering pyramid of boxed crackers, which came tumbling down everywhere, bombarding an innocent customer who was pushing her cart from the opposite direction. "Help! Help!" the woman screamed, surprised by the avalanche of boxes.

A crowd had gathered instantly. Abby saw that Dawn was trying to calm the woman. "What happened? Tell me what happened," Dawn kept asking. The woman gasped, shook her head, and pointed toward the wrecked display. "That could have killed me. Where's the manager? Get me the manager!"

"He's not here right now," Dawn said. "I'm in charge. I'm sorry this happened. It's an unfortunate accident."

As if on cue, the door opened and a man who turned out to be Mr. Grey, the store manager, entered. He was small in stature, but he had a big voice. "What's going on here? Dawn, what's this all about? I left you in charge."

Dawn looked stricken. "Oh, Mr. Grey, I don't know. I . . ." She was near tears. "I'm so sorry. It was quiet in here, and then . . ."

Dawn was interrupted by the woman, who had finally gotten herself under control. "I'll sue," she said loudly. "I'll sue. My lawyers will contact you!" Then she pushed her way out of the crowd and disappeared out the door.

Abby looked at Dawn's face, and whatever humor she had seen in the situation suddenly disappeared. This prank had gotten out of hand and wasn't funny. Abby expected Bill to say something. Wiping what seemed to be tears of laughter away from his eyes, he suddenly drew a very serious look on his face and walked toward the cash register. "I think I can explain," Abby said. "You see, it wasn't Dawn's fault. I'm sorry, I guess I'm to blame. I wasn't paying attention and my cart accidentally hit your display. I'd be willing to tell anyone my story or sign anything that will help you with that woman's lawyer."

Mr. Grey squinted, looked at Abby, and said, "Come into my office."

Mr. Levin approached the manager and said, "I'm the young woman's teacher. We're here as part of a field trip. I think I had better come, too."

Mr. Grey nodded, and the three of them went to the back of the store.

The crowd dispersed. Finally, Mr. Levin reappeared with Abby. The group paid for their groceries. As Abby helped fit the bags into one of the carts, she looked and saw Bill wink at her. He was not the least bit upset. Abby felt furious toward Bill but even more angry with herself. Maybe she was to blame—after all, she had jumped off the cart and Bill probably couldn't stop it. But she couldn't figure out what it was about Bill that had convinced her to hop on the cart in the first place.

As Abby was loading her car, Marilyn walked over to help her. "Are you sure you're to blame for that fiasco?" Marilyn asked.

"Well," Abby paused, "it was an accident. Anyhow, what do you mean?"

"Hmmm," Marilyn answered. "Things always seem to get out of hand when Bill Kelsey is around.

I hope he's not going to screw up this trip. I hate show-offs."

"Well, no real harm was done. The lady will probably calm down and realize that it wasn't the store's fault. Mr. Grey can see that Dawn wasn't to blame. After all is said and done, it was kind of absurd."

"Yeah, some laugh," Marilyn said. "I can't believe Bill wasn't involved."

"You know, when the boxes came down and the lady was screaming it was like a movie—for a while," Abby said as she got into the driver's seat of her car and turned on the engine.

"I guess so," said Marilyn. "I just hope Bill doesn't think he has to give us a lot of laughs while we're out on the road. See you tomorrow."

"Can I give you a ride?" Abby asked. "I have to drop the food you'll be carrying at your house sometime. Why not now?"

"No thanks. I have to do a few more errands."

"Fine. See you later on today," Abby replied, and she pulled out of the parking lot.

On the way home, Abby thought about the scene. Bill hadn't even come up to her to say anything. As she drove along, she said aloud to the empty car, "All right, all right, pranks are dumb, but Bill won't do anything like that while we're on the trip. He wouldn't do anything stupid and dangerous. He didn't take responsibility because we both didn't need to get in trouble, and then it would have looked like a prank. I'm sure he'll apologize to me."

Abby shifted the car into low and drove up the

steep hill that ran toward her house, glad that she had decided to limit her thoughts to the prospect of tomorrow's adventure. "I haven't thought about Buddy all morning," she said to herself. "So there, Buddy."

4

Mr. Levin greeted the group of eight shivering cyclists who waited for him in the high-school parking lot. "We're all here promptly this time, I see. Good." He looked at the gear piled near the waiting bikes and added, "I know that you've all packed, but there are still a couple of things that have to go along with us—the stove and a first-aid kit. They can't be added to one person's gear easily, but I've rigged them so that they can be tied onto a backpack. We'll take turns carrying them. They're really not all that heavy, just cumbersome."

"Are you kidding?" Dale asked plaintively. "I already feel like there's a mountain on top of me. My tires are flat from all the weight they're carrying."

"I understand, Dale," Mr. Levin said patiently, "but this stuff has just got to go along. You won't have to carry anything extra in the beginning. I'll give you some time to get used to the pace but you'll have to carry them some time. We're all going to have to pitch in."

"All right," Dale mumbled. "If I have to."

"You do," Mr. Levin said. "I'll carry the stove

first, and Mitchell, can I ask you to haul the first-
aid kit?"

"Sure, Mr. Levin, my pleasure," Mitch answered.

"Let's see you be so cheery after you've carried it
for twenty miles or so," said Dale, but Mitchell paid
him no attention as he strapped the bulky kit onto
his backpack.

"All right," said Mr. Levin. "Looks like we're all
ready. Just follow the rules of the road, and remember, no riding two abreast whenever there is anything more than very light traffic. One last thing
before we leave. Who's the boss?"

"You're the boss!" the eight cyclists roared in
response.

"Good. Remember to remember that, too." Mr.
Levin checked his watch, and then said, "As they
used to say in those old cowboy movies, 'Let's mount
up!'"

The nine riders left the blacktopped parking lot
and soon had maneuvered their way through the
downtown traffic to the edge of town. The pace of
the ride was slow. Traffic lights and stop signs hind-
ered their progress, and Abby felt herself getting
impatient. The sun peered down through a morning
haze and warmed her just enough so that she wondered if she was going to be overdressed when she
really started to exercise. She decided to worry about
that when the time came. Right now she was feeling
fine and was excited because the trip had begun.

They came to the town line, and Mr. Levin sig-
naled a halt. "Well, how are you doing so far?" he
asked.

Marilyn laughed. "Considering that we've gone

all of three miles in stop-and-go traffic, we're doing fine. How are you holding up?"

"Don't worry. I'll make it. I just wanted to stop here because once we hit the main road up ahead, we're not going to be starting and stopping anymore. It's now eight-thirty. I think we should stop for a snack at about ten, and then, depending on where we are, I figure on a lunch break at about twelve-thirty. We'll get into the exploration of nature this afternoon when we've reached interesting country. For this first part of the ride, I'll bring up the rear. Mitchell, would you take the lead for the first leg? Weighted down with the first-aid kit, you won't be able to get too far out in front or go too fast for the rest of us. We don't want to break any speed records, right?"

"Best believe it," said Dale. "As you know, I'm not in the best shape in the world."

"You'll be fine, Dale," Mr. Levin said. "You just need to build some self-confidence along with your muscles." He looked at Mitchell. "All set?" he asked.

Mitch nodded, and Mr. Levin said, "Then let's go."

"Now this is more like it," Marilyn said half an hour later as she pulled even with Abby. "I don't think Mr. Levin will mind if we ride side-by-side here. There's no traffic."

"I think it's fine." Abby smiled. "But I'm not sure I'll be able to talk and pedal at the same time!"

"You know, Abby," Marilyn hesitated. "I found what you said at the orientation meeting about the stars interesting. I guess it's always been fascinating to me too, but I'm embarrassed to talk about it!"

"I know what you mean," Abby answered. "But I've overcome my embarrassment. Everybody in the Zodiac Club has."

"Well—everybody at Collingwood High knows about the Zodiac Club. But are you allowed to tell me more about it? I thought it was a secret sorority."

Abby had to take a few seconds to get her breath as they pedaled up a long, slow incline. When she was able to speak, Abby answered, "It's not a secret club, but it's not public like a school club either. The group of us got together last summer when we were planning a birthday party for Cathy Rosen. Do you know her?"

Marilyn nodded.

Abby continued. "I guess I was the one who promoted the zodiac idea. I thought that using star compatibility would be a great theme for her party. You know, how to find the perfect boy—the one who is compatible with your star sign. Anyway, we used the zodiac, but I don't just believe it for those reasons. It's an ancient science."

Their conversation was interrupted by a message sent forward by Mr. Levin. Dale called that they were to separate and ride single file because the road narrowed ahead.

Marilyn called as she dropped behind Abby, "To be continued. By the way, who's compatible with my sign?"

Abby smiled and said, "Give me some time to think about that."

She felt incredibly happy. After the long winter of dark days and being indoors, it felt wonderful to be outdoors, not thinking of anything of importance and feeling the blood pound through her veins. There was, she realized once more, something special about this time of the year when winter gradually gave way to spring. It was as if the world and everything in it was coming out of a deep sleep. It's like the earth is reawakening, she thought. Then she made a face as she realized that what she was thinking was one of the oldest clichés in the book. However, in a few seconds she smiled again. Who cared if it was a cliché? It was true, and it made her feel so good, special, and alive. The steady rhythm of her legs as they pumped the bike's pedals became a background to her high spirits, and she began to hum to herself as she rode along. Now that they were started, Abby felt confident the trip was going to be a fabulous success. Mara was right. Marilyn was really a good kid. Abby felt that she would have a wonderfully inspiring experience when she got to the top of Ram's Head Mountain, especially since she was an Aries. She wondered about her Zodiac friends. If only they could see how happy she was— but she was feeling too good to dwell for long on what the others might be doing or what she might be missing.

Time passed, and the group biked farther and farther into the countryside. Patches of snow could still be seen streaking the fields, and the sun played hide and seek with the clouds. It was pretty, yet fragile, and hinted at mystery. Abby took a breath and felt content.

Her feeling of euphoria soon gave way to that of hunger. Abby checked her watch. Nine-fifty. Good. She was ready for a little rest and a slug of something sweet to replace the calories she had burned up in the hour and a half of strenuous riding.

They came to a rest stop on the road. Mr. Levin sent word to the front of the line that Mitchell should stop.

One after another, they pulled in and dismounted.

"How are you doin', Abby?" Mitchell asked as she shrugged off her pack.

"Great. I feel absolutely great. Isn't this fun?"

Mitchell nodded in agreement, "I haven't felt so great since I went backpacking in Mexico this past summer."

"You were in Mexico backpacking?" Abby asked, not hiding her surprise.

Mitchell laughed. "Yeah, I was. I'm not chained to a computer or a chemistry lab, you know. I do other things with my life. You might be surprised . . ."

"I didn't mean . . ." Abby hesitated. "I only thought that you were more of . . ."

". . . The indoor, studious type," Mitchell finished for her. "I am. I am also the outdoor, fresh-air type. I just don't like organized athletics. Who wins or loses on the playing fields of old Collingwood High just doesn't fascinate me."

Tom had joined them. "I think that's a mistake," he said. "After all, competitive sports are a great training ground for life. We compete all the time, for grades, for jobs, for girls."

"I didn't say I wasn't competitive," Mitchell said. "I just don't like competitive team sports, that's all. I like to choose the arenas I compete in." He turned toward Abby, "Winning and losing is important. But kicking or catching a ball just doesn't count in the same way as, lets say, competing for a girl's affection."

At that moment Mr. Levin arrived, followed by a flushed and panting Dale Chambers.

Wouldn't you know it, Abby thought to herself. When I finally get Mitchell talking about something interesting, Mr. Levin and Dale show up.

"Hey, you guys," Dale puffed. "I thought that you were going to take it easy. I . . . I . . ." he paused and tried to catch his breath. "I'm having a little trouble keeping up, and we just started. Can you . . . slow the pace a little?"

"Oh brother," sighed Tracey from where she sat. "We're never going to get to Ram's Head if we have to go at a snail's pace."

"That's enough, Tracey," Mr. Levin warned. "I think that it's only right that we show Dale some consideration. He'll get more stamina as we go along, I'm sure."

"I know what we can do to speed you up, Dale," said Bill. "I'll ride right in front of you with a roast beef sandwich taped to my back. That will spur you on, won't it? And every time you are just about to reach out and grab it, I'll speed up. That will get us all to Ram's Head in no time."

"Oh, Bill's too much." Fannie giggled.

"Come on, give Dale a break," Abby found herself piping up. "We're *all* supposed to have fun on this trip. Maybe we can take it a little slower between now and lunch. Then we can readjust our speed later."

"Why don't you take the lead and set the pace, Abby?" said Mr. Levin.

"Sorry, I didn't realize . . ." Mitchell began.

"You did well, Mitchell." Mr. Levin reached out and patted him lightly on the shoulder. "We'll just change positions. Now, who's ready for a few carbs?" he said as he held up a big bag of chocolate chip cookies.

The cookies were shared. The nine of them sat and silently savored the sweet treats. Abby enjoyed the silence and happily munched way. When Mr. Levin passed around a comb of real honey, she thought that she had never tasted anything so good. The wax in the comb reminded her of red lips she used to buy at Halloween. She remembered chewing until all the flavor was gone and her jaw started to ache. She thought of trick-or-treat with Cathy. Now Cathy was with the girls at Penny's house and she was alone. She took down her canteen and had a long slug. The water tasted delicious and she threw her head back to breathe in the sweet spring air. The sun came out from behind a cloud and shone directly upon her, and she felt more relaxed. I *am* determined to be happy, Abby thought. I'll remember this trip for years!

Mr. Levin broke the silence. "Sorry to interrupt your daydreams, but we've got ground to cover. Pace or no pace, I'm hoping we can cover ten miles before we stop for lunch. I have a spot near Hawk's Landing all picked out that will allow us to have a good look at some interesting lichen. I hope you've noticed the trees we've been passing."

"Well, then, let's get going," Tracey said. "If I

stay here much longer, I may just want to pitch camp and not move again."

They all got up, stretched, and got on their bikes. Abby set a moderate pace, and Dale seemed to keep up. Even so, it took longer than anticipated to reach Hawk's Landing.

"Cold cuts this afternoon for lunch," Marilyn said, "but tonight we'll all pitch in and make a hot meal, fit for a king."

"The way to a man's heart is through his stomach, right, Marilyn?" Tracey asked.

"Sounds good to me," said Bill. "I bet Abby, Fannie, Marilyn, and even Tracey are the Julia Childs of the great outdoors."

"Not so fast, Kelsey," Marilyn replied. "Mr. Levin said we would *all* help make the meal."

"What?" he replied. His eyes widened as he laughed. "Isn't cooking women's work?"

"Only if chopping all the firewood for cooking and the campfire is men's work," Abby answered.

"I'll cook. I'll cook," Bill said, throwing up his hands in a gesture of resignation.

Abby smiled. I wonder what his sign is, she mused. I'll bet he's a Scorpio. They are strong willed and use that strength to manipulate other people.

After lunch, Mr. Levin led them on a lichen expedition. Marilyn volunteered to lead next. "I don't know how good I'll be at setting a pace, but I'll try. How many miles should we try to cover this afternoon?"

"If we could make another ten or so by the time the sun gets ready to set, we'd be in good shape," Mr. Levin answered.

"Oh, my aching legs! Oh, my poor back!" Dale exclaimed. "I may die before we get to eat dinner."

"Oh, come on, Dale," said Marilyn, throwing an arm around the overweight boy's shoulder. "It sounds much worse than it really is. You can do it—you're doing well now. Your mother will be proud."

Dale, obviously pleased by the attention from such a good-looking girl, gave a small grimace and said, "Okay, I'll try."

They set off again with Abby following close behind Marilyn.

Abby observed that Marilyn obviously relished her leadership role as much as Abby did. Could she be an Aries, Abby wondered. No, she's more like a Capricorn.

By the time the sun had begun to set, Mr. Levin passed word from the rear that they only had a mile to go before they reached the spot where he wanted to stop.

Before long they came to a small path to the right of the highway. "Take that right," Mr. Levin called out. Marilyn obeyed. Soon the whole group arrived at a small clearing with a rustic campsite.

"Looks great, Mr. Levin," Mitchell said as he took off his backpack and tried to get the kinks out of his back.

"Mitch, you carried the first-aid kit all day today," Mr. Levin said as he watched the boy stretch. "I forgot to switch it."

"It's okay, Mr. Levin," Mitchell answered. "It really wasn't much of a bother, and I thought some of the others really would have been slowed down if they carried it."

"Well, all right, but you make sure that someone else carries it tomorrow," Mr. Levin said seriously. Then he announced, "Time to set up and cook! Let's all gather wood for the fire. The menu for tonight is stone soup!"

"What?" asked Tracey incredulously.

Mr. Levin smiled. "Stone soup, and you'll like it."

Tracey made a face. "Eating stones may be your idea of gourmet food, but I'm tired and hungry. Biking with my boyfriend is one thing, this is another."

"Tracey, Tracey, where is your sense of adventure?" Mr. Levin shook his head. "For that matter, where are your childhood memories?"

"What do you mean?" Fannie asked, as if coming to Tracey's rescue.

"I know what Mr. Levin's talking about," Mitch said. "Don't you remember the story? Two hungry soldiers arrived in a town and asked for food, but the greedy villagers wouldn't give them any. The soldiers were clever, so they asked for a pot, filled it with water, and added a stone. After the water was hot, they tasted it and said it was delicious. The villager were curious about how such a soup could possibly taste good, and they asked if they could sample it. The soldiers said they'd be glad to share their soup, but to make it *really* scrumptious, it needed some onions. One of the villagers ran off and got the onions and added them."

"Now I remember," said Abby. "The soldiers taste the soup again and say it's just about right, but that some beef stock might make it a soup that no one in the village would ever forget, so someone gets the stock. The soldiers repeat this four more times, asking for carrots, potatoes, and more. Finally, they let the villagers taste the soup. The villagers are amazed. The soup is wonderful. Everyone agrees that soup made from a stone is quite the best kind of soup in the world."

"That's right, Abby," said Mr. Levin.

"You get an A in fairy tales," added Mitchell.

"You lead the way, Mitch. You're tonight's chef," Mr. Levin said with a smile.

The cooking went well. Dale almost burned the biscuits, but by the time they were ready to eat, everyone was so hungry they didn't mind the charred taste. Dale suggested that the burned spots added a little *"je ne sais quoi"* to the meal, and Bill replied, "I know exactly what it adds, pure carbon." Everybody laughed. The group found itself relaxing, and for the first time since they had come together, enjoying each other's company.

There was much joking and fooling around as they cleaned up. When Mr. Levin started to sing, "Down by the Old Mill Stream," they all joined in. Then Marilyn started "I Want a Girl Just Like the Girl," and Bill followed with the take-off on it, "I Want a Beer Just Like the Beer."

They soon had a song fest going. They gathered around the fire and sang for half an hour. The night was lit by moon and stars. It was chilly, but the fire and good mood that settled over the group helped keep everyone feeling warm and content. Mr. Levin began an informal lecture on the greenery they would see during the miles to come.

"Tomorrow morning," he said, "we'll begin to study Mother Nature. Now one more song. How about 'Row, Row, Row Your Boat'?"

"I haven't sung songs like that since I was a Girl Scout," Abby said. "We went on overnights to Camp Wind in the Pines." She sighed contentedly, and a silence fell over the group.

"We've had a long day and we've another one ahead of us tomorrow. Let's get ready to hit the hay, but I have to say I think this is a group that's not afraid to interact, appreciate nature and each other. We only have a couple of days, but I think if we go around the campfire and each one of us tells the group something that the rest of the group doesn't know . . ."

Bill Kelsey let out a groan. "Here we go with that touchy-feely stuff," he said.

"No, not really," Mr. Levin replied. "You can share a small detail of your life, just as long as what you say is true. We're together on a trip like this so let's know more about each other than we did before we left. How about it?"

"I'm game, I guess," Fannie said nervously. All the others, except for Bill, agreed.

"Just like the last time we compared notes," Mr. Levin began. "I'll go first to break the ice. Let's see . . . One of the reasons I organized this biking expedition is that it's athletic, but no one is put into a win-lose position against anyone but oneself. In my teen years, people had expectations that I would be a great athlete because I look like one, but I preferred not to meet other people's goals for me. I made my own! I became a cyclist because of the pleasure I can give myself."

"That's interesting," said Tom. "Mitchell and I were talking this afternoon. You know, when you're a teenager it's hard to think that teachers or parents were like us when they were young. Remember," he said speaking quickly, "what I said about coming on this trip? About college applications and all of that? If I had my way, I wouldn't go to college at all. I really like woodworking. My dad has a good shop in our basement, and he's helped me to do some really fine things. What I'd like to do is to apprentice myself to someone who makes fabulous furniture. My dad says that woodworking is fine as a hobby, but that no one can earn any real money at it. Furniture is mass produced, and I guess he's right, only . . ." Tom stopped talking and gazed raptly into the fire. "Well, I guess I said something honest about myself."

After a few seconds, Tracey spoke up. "Here's something which should give everyone a good laugh. I come from a very strict and religious family. I think my mother actually used to dream that I'd become a nun. I've been crazy about dance since I was a little girl. I still take ballet lessons—that's why it's easy for me to cycle. I'm limber, but I know that I'm not prima ballerina material. However, I love it—the grace, the costumes, the music. Since I can't do classical ballet, I want to do showgirl stuff. You know, like the Rockettes or *Chorus Line*. The problem, of course, is my parents. They think the life of a dancer is wild and terrible. What's a girl to do?"

"If Tracey can tell you that, then here's something

about me," Dale said. "I love animals. They're so different from people—much nicer, I think. I want to be a vet when I get out of college." He fell silent, then added, "Animals don't care if you're overweight."

"Is that all?" Bill asked as if he didn't believe it.

"Mr. Levin said we didn't have to say a lot, just what was true," Dale answered. "I want to be a vet, so I told you."

"Sorry," Bill said, and shrugged his shoulders. "I didn't mean anything."

"I'll go next," Marilyn said. "It's kind of serious, but it's no big secret." She took a breath. "I had a twin sister who died. Her name was Helen. She died when we were babies, so I don't even remember her. But I feel as if I have to do everything for both of us."

"That's so sad," Abby said.

"It's as if I have to accomplish for two. Maybe to make it up to my parents that she died. My parents and I have talked it over. They say that I shouldn't feel the way I do and that I shouldn't put too much pressure on myself, but I just can't seem to stop."

The group around the fire grew silent.

Suddenly Bill began, "As for me, I was born to poor, but honest, pig farmers in Iowa. A band of traveling accountants stole me away because, as my father always tells me, accountants are molded, not born, and wouldn't it be a good idea if I started thinking about the bright future I might have in the family accounting firm."

"Come on, Bill, Mr. Levin said that we had to

tell the truth. You weren't born on a pig farm," Fannie said.

"No, Fannie," Bill sighed. "I was not. I was just trying to take a bit of the chill off. I thought that I'd tell my story in a way that might provide a laugh."

"We laughed, but do you have anything to say besides the fact that you don't want to be a boring accountant like your father and join his firm?" asked Tracey as if Bill had made a mistake.

"No, I don't," Bill said. "I have no sad or moving stories to tell. I just want a few laughs. One day at a time, and what you see is what you get."

"Bill," Mr. Levin began, "I think . . ."

"No, I'm all through, Mr. Levin," Bill said. "You said 'volunteer.' I hate this tell-and-become-my-best-friend stuff. So let's go on to someone who is more self-analytical. How about you, Fannie Green? What's your little truth?"

For once, Fannie didn't giggle. She looked directly at Bill. "My 'little' truth is kind of big deal to me. I just want to say that I'm really happy to be on this trip because I'm being treated as an equal. I am the youngest of five kids, so my family treats me like the baby. They don't mean to, but they do. I am *so* tired of being treated like a baby and being angry about it and pretending I'm not. It's only because my parents know Mr. Levin—he was my older brother's teacher—that they allowed me to come. I'm so used to being treated like a silly girl that I sometimes just act like one."

There was a short pause, and then Mr. Levin said,

"Two more to be heard from. How about you, Mitchell?"

Mitchell hesitated. "I could make something up, and you'd probably never know the difference, but that would be cheating somehow," he explained. "I . . . I guess the thing that very few people know about me is that I'm ambitious. Maybe ambitious is the wrong word, but it's as close as I can come. I don't mean by the word that I just want to succeed. Well, I do want to succeed, of course, but I want something else. If my life can be seen as a jar, I want to fill that jar up to the top. I want to feel things, and know things, and do things that I can't even imagine now. I guess people see me as a 'type.' We all like to make the kids we know fit into one of the categories we know about: the jock, the wise guy, the brain. At this point, I may be more one type than the other, but I don't want to be that all my life. I want so much, or at least to try for it. Whew," Mitchell laughed, "you shouldn't have put that nickel in, Mr. Levin. I spoke too much."

Abby looked across the fire to where Mitchell sat. He looked a bit flustered, but he looked *alive*. She had never seen him in that way before. He looked almost handsome. It flickered across her mind that she really ought to pay some attention to him. He'd be a nice guy to know. Maybe she *wouldn't* introduce him to Jessica—she'd keep him to herself. Then she remembered Buddy.

"How about you, Abby?" Mr. Levin asked.

"I shouldn't have waited to go last," Abby replied, "because what I have to say is that the vernal equinox, the day we are due at Ram's Head—I know I said this already—is also the first day of my sign, Aries. I really feel pulled to see the sun come up from that particular mountain on that precise day. I know that lots of people laugh at astrology and don't consider it a real science, but somewhere deep inside me, I know that it has some truth to it. There are good and bad things about myself that I just can't help but believe are influenced by the stars."

"Astrology isn't real science, although scientists do feel the tides are affected by the moon," Mitchell said. "And if you're an Aries, you'd better be careful on this trip."

"What do you mean?" Abby asked, puzzled.

"I know some astrology, and Aries are always in danger of hurting themselves. We wouldn't want you falling off your bike like Jack and Jill and go tumbling down one of these mighty steep hills and splitting your head open."

Abby looked at Mitchell in amazement. "How did you know that? Is Aries your sign, too?"

He laughed. "No, it isn't. I'm an Aquarius, born on the fourth of February. Can't you tell? I have an inquisitive nature. According to the astrology books, I'm prone to give serious consideration to new ideas. I guess that's why I'm here on this adventure."

"Come on. You're making fun of my favorite pastime," Abby joked. "I'll tell you what an expert I am—Abby Martin—leading light of the Zodiac Club. From what you said at our pretrip meeting, I guessed that you were a conservative Cancer. I should have waited to get to know you better before I made my decision."

"Does that mean your picture of me has improved?" asked Mitchell with a pleased look on his face. "But I'm not sure I buy all this personality matching with your sign. I think you can find something that fits everyone if you read enough astrology books."

"Gosh," Abby sighed. "You sound just like my father—a real skeptic."

"You're right," Mitchell replied. "I'd much rather stick with astronomy and watch the stars move in the sky."

"Well," said Tracey, "you two can stay up and talk about the stars and your compatibility, but I'm about to fall asleep, and I'm starting to feel cold. Is it all right to climb into our sleeping bags, Mr. Levin?"

"Of course, Tracey. Good idea. Tom, please help me dig the pit a bit deeper around the fire, will you? We'll get up about seven o'clock. We've got another long day ahead of us tomorrow. See you in the A.M."

They murmured their good-nights and unrolled their sleeping bags.

Suddenly the day's activities caught up with Abby and she felt completely exhausted. She crawled into her sleeping bag, curled into a ball, and shut her eyes. As she drifted off to sleep, she found herself thinking about what she had heard around the campfire. As usual, Bill didn't take anything seriously. Only he wouldn't be honest about himself. Mitchell was definitely interesting. She liked what he said about filling his life up to the top. So he was an Aquarius. Abby wondered how compatible an air

sign was with a fire sign like Aries. It was terrific
to find a boy who would, at least, talk about astrology, even if he didn't believe in it. As for Tracey,
the ballet dancer . . . wait until she told Mara about
the Viper's family. Marilyn's story was a tragic one.
Abby felt sad, but before she could gather another
thought, sleep overtook her.

Abby stood in a dark cave. She tried to move forward, but her feet were somehow bound together. The cave's chilling cold seemed to envelope her face like a mask. With every breath she took, her ears and nose seemed to grow colder. She turned her head and buried it against the side of the cave, now suddenly grown soft and warm.

As if from out of another dimension, a dull knife appeared and poked her in the ribs. Abby turned one way and then another, but there was no escaping the knife's point. Frantic, she twisted. Then she heard her name. If she could get to the person who was calling her, the torment would be over. She had to try, she had to.

"Abby, Abby, wake up." It was Fannie whispering.

Abby opened her eyes. "What? Who?" She had been dreaming. Her sleeping bag was twisted around her, and she realized Fannie was poking her. Next to her Marilyn slept heavily, a little snore sometimes escaping her lips.

Abby whispered hoarsely, "Fannie, it's dark out,

66

and didn't anyone ever teach you how to wake some one gently? My ribs are sore! What in the devil do you want?"

"I'm sorry, Abby, but somebody's out there."

"What?"

"Somebody's out there in the woods. Listen."

Abby listened and heard nothing. "Really, Fannie, it's too early," she said as she turned over and started to go back to sleep.

"Don't go back to sleep, Abby," Fannie begged. "Just wait a minute, you'll hear it."

From her left side, Abby heard Tracey's sleepy voice. "Will you two pipe down? It's the middle of the night for goodness sake! I'm trying to sleep!"

Then from out of the dark came a sound that was halfway between a whistle and a sob. It sounded vaguely as if a small child were crying.

Fannie gave a small cry herself and said, "See?"

Abby was still not fully awake, but she felt a small shiver of fear run down her back. Tracey sat bolt upright and said, "What's that?"

"Shhh. I don't know," Abby answered. "Be quiet."

Silence fell again. There was no moon in the sky and the pines around the campground sighed as a cold breeze ran through them. The fire flickered, and Abby strained her eyes to see into the dark. It was difficult to tell where the sound had come from. There had to be an explanation. If she could just associate the sound with something familiar, she knew everything would be all right. She looked across the fire to where the boys were sleeping. Nobody stirred. All the sleeping bags were motionless.

Then the small, piercing cry came again, and
Fannie called, "Mr. Levin!"

"Shut up!" Tracey commanded. "Do you want to
wake everybody up and have them think we're
wimps?"

"But I'm scared," Fannie said.

"Don't be scared. It's probably just some animal,"
Abby said. "It'll probably go away."

The three girls waited for another call. The woods
were silent.

"This is one time Abby was right," Tracey whispered. She looked at her watch. "It's three-thirty.
Can we *please* go back to sleep now?" She lay down
and pulled her sleeping bag up to her nose. Abby
and Fannie looked around once more, then followed
Tracey's example.

Abby couldn't sleep. Images from the movies, in
which a crazed killer came crashing through the
woods and slaughtered a band of teenagers, raced
through her mind. Ridiculous, she thought. What
mad killer would be after us?

Abby felt her muscles tightening. She freed an
arm from her sleeping bag and peered at her watch.
Maybe dawn would come soon. She sighed. Only
ten minutes had gone by since she had lain down
again.

A log fell off the pile by the campfire with a
bump. Abby sat up with a start.

Where was the killer?

Was he already in the camp?

Should she warn the others?

Abby looked left and right once again and saw

that Fannie was also sitting up and looking out into the dark.

"This is ridiculous," Abby whispered across Marilyn.

"Let's just *go to sleep*!" Tracey said.

Just as Abby was putting her head down, she heard two short, high-pitched cries through the woods. At the edge of the clearing, a broad-shouldered man appeared! He tugged at his belt and took a step toward the sleeping boys.

As the form began to draw nearer, Abby felt herself paralyzed with fear, but Fannie put her head back and screamed, "No! No! No! Don't hurt us, please!"

At once, the camp became an uproar. Tom, as if prodded by an electric shock, jumped up and assumed a martial arts stance. Tracey clutched her sleeping bag to her chest and joined Fannie's screams with a long, sirenlike one of her own. Dale, still in his sleeping bag, curled into a ball and put his hands over his head. Marilyn awoke from a deep sleep and struggled to sit up.

Mr. Levin and Mitchell jumped to their feet, grabbed their flashlights, and came running to the girls' aid.

The intruder realized that Fannie was pointing toward him and called out, "Hey, what's going on. What did I do? I was being quiet. It's me, Bill. I didn't mean . . ."

Abby felt a surge of relief flood over her. She began to laugh, and the more she thought about it, the harder she laughed. No one else was laughing and she realized they were staring at her.

"I'm sorry. It's not funny. We, we woke you up, and . . ." she began to laugh again. "Oh, oh . . . it's the middle of the night. I thought that we were in *Halloween, Part Four.* It's so silly, but . . ."

"Slow down and tell the rest of us what's going on," said Mr. Levin.

"Mr. Levin, it's my fault, I think," Fannie said. "I got Abby and Tracey all worked up because I heard something, and then when Bill walked into the clearing, it was so scary I thought he was a killer and I started screaming."

"Can't a guy heed the call of nature?" Bill asked of no one in particular. "All I did was get up and go into the woods. I didn't expect to start a riot."

"I'm sorry, Bill. I really am," said Abby, who was getting control of herself. "We heard this weird noise, and I guess our imaginations just started running wild."

"What kind of sound?" Mr. Levin asked.

"It was like somebody giving a strange sort of chuckle or little scream," Tracey said. "I never heard anything like it before. Abby said that it was an animal. She was probably right, but it didn't sound like any animal I ever heard. It sounded like a lunatic out there."

"It sounds as though it might have been a young screech owl." Mitchell said. "They *do* sound weird the first time you hear them. I don't blame you for getting frightened."

"Why didn't anyone else wake up?" asked Tracey in an annoyed tone. "You could have told us what it was."

"Just good sleepers, I guess," Mitchell replied.

"The noise made me start thinking of all those stupid horror pictures I've seen," Abby continued, "and when we saw a form in the moonlight, it was like a nightmare coming true."

"I just started to scream. I'm sorry," Fannie said.

Mr. Levin stretched. "I'm sorry that you girls got scared. You should have wakened me right away."

"Fannie wanted to, but we wouldn't let her," Abby said. "We didn't want to act like wimps."

"So you acted like fire sirens instead," Mr. Levin said. "Well, it's over now. I say we all go back to sleep. If any more mad killers show up, please wake me. Otherwise, see you in the morning." He ambled back to his sleeping bag.

Feeling embarrassed but relieved, Abby got back into her sleeping bag. Marilyn had already gotten into hers and was settling down. Soon Tracey and Fannie joined the other girls.

"I'm sorry to have gotten you up, Marilyn. I really am," Fannie said.

"Don't worry about it. Just let me get back to sleep now." Marilyn said groggily.

"Sure. Good night, Abby."

"Good night, Fannie. We really were awfully silly."

"I know. Good night, Tracey."

"Good night, Fan."

The camp was silent. Then from where the boys were lying came a cackle. Soft at first, then louder, like the laugh of a crazy man.

Abby shifted in her sleeping bag, closed her eyes, and called out, "Not funny, you guys, not funny at all." Then she turned on her side and fell into a dreamless sleep.

"Rise and shine. Rise and shine." Mr. Levin stood in the center of the campground and bellowed in a way that Abby found disgustingly cheerful. It was warm in her sleeping bag, and she could feel the cold morning air nipping at her nose. It would be much nicer to stay rolled up like a hibernating animal than to "rise and shine." Finally, Abby crawled out of her bag and rubbed her eyes. "Well, at least the sun's shining," she said to Tracey, who was standing next to her.

Mitchell, who was busy tending the newly built fire, said, "Yeah, but I don't like the looks of it. Too bright, and look at that haze surrounding the sun. That old saying, 'Red sky at morning, sailors take warning,' seems right for today."

"Mitchell," Marilyn said with a flirtatious note in her voice, "you may be right, but at least it isn't raining. Do you have to be so pessimistic?"

Mitchell shrugged and shot her a good-natured smile. Then he turned and silently gave the fire his full attention.

The other members of the group slowly emerged from their sleeping bags, splashed their faces with water from their canteens, and then disappeared into the woods, boys to the right, girls to the left. Finally, everyone was standing around the fire waiting for the scrambled eggs and coffee that Mr. Levin and Fannie had volunteered to make.

Bill stood near Abby. "Any more ghosts or killers last night?" he asked.

"Not a one, I'm happy to report," she answered.

"Good. Well, here we are. Another day, another set of sore muscles."

"Really?" Abby replied. "I thought Dale was the one who was supposed to be in lousy shape. Your body beautiful looks as if it could stand up to a ride like this."

"I can see you have good taste in bodies," he said. "I work out with weights, but that doesn't develop the same kind of muscles you need for this kind of exercise. Look at Mitchell. He's not what anyone would call Superman, but he doesn't seem to be having any trouble with this trip. I haven't seen him slow his pace at all, and he's not limping around the way I am this morning. Anyway," Bill continued, looking at Abby directly, "I was meant to be a lover, not an athlete." Then he gave her arm a small squeeze. But before Abby had a chance to say anything, he moved to the other side of the fire and began a conversation with Tom.

Abby felt both confused and pleasantly surprised. The eggs she had just eaten seemed to do a flip-flop in her stomach. Surely, Bill hadn't meant anything deeply personal in what he had just said. Then why had he squeezed her arm? Was this trip going to turn into something more than she had planned? Abby looked across the fire to where Bill was standing. He seemed engrossed in what he was saying, but when she glanced back again a few moments later, she found herself looking into his devilish eyes. What's wrong with me? she wondered. Part of me wants to avoid Bill, and part of me can't stop thinking about him.

"All right now, let's wash the frying pan and utensils. Then put out the fire, and we can be on our way," Mr. Levin announced. "There's a sheer wall up ahead about twelve miles or so, and I want to stop there to show you a colony of swallows that have improvised some amazing nest formations. We'll leave here in about six minutes. Tracey, I'd like you to take the lead this morning."

"But, Mr. Levin, I got a lousy night's sleep, and my legs ache," Tracey whined.

"We all had a lousy night's sleep, thanks to the phantom killer, and your legs won't ache once you get going. Take it slow at first, and you'll find that you'll be warmed up and speeding along in no time." Mr. Levin reached out and gave Tracey's shoulder a quick squeeze. "We all ache a bit, you know," he said.

Abby thought to herself, See, dummy, people touch each other all the time, and they don't mean anything by it. Mr. Levin was not coming on to Tracey, and Bill Kelsey is not coming on to you. Forget it, and ride in the morning sun.

Mr. Levin's advice to Tracey proved correct. Soon after they were back on the road, the group was equaling the speed they had attained the day before. There was a cooler, damper feel to the air, but Abby didn't mind it. They were definitely climbing higher into the hills. If I feel this good now, Abby thought, wait until I'm at the top of Ram's Head. It's going to be excellent! What a story I'll be able to tell the Zodiacs.

Before long, they came to the place Mr. Levin had mentioned.

"Stop here and look up!" he shouted.

Abby did what he ordered and saw a strange and spectacular sight. Rising up from the left-hand side of the road for what seemed at least sixty yards was a sheer cliff of gray stone. It reminded Abby of a fairy tale she had once read about a glass mountain on which a princess sat waiting for someone to rescue her. However, this was not the cold, isolated mountain of the story. From all around the sheer gray cliff, hundreds of swallows darted and swooped, calling to each other in high-pitched voices.

As the birds flew toward the mountainside, they seemed to disappear, then reappear from inside the rocks. Abby could see no way for the hundreds of birds to get a perch on the sheer cliff. The sight of their darting to and fro filled her with wonder.

"It's amazing, isn't it?" Mr. Levin asked.

"It sure is," Dale replied. "Where do they go?"

"You can't see it from here, but the face of the cliff is covered with small fissures, and the swallows have ingeniously built their nests inside those very small cracks. The nests are absolutely safe from predators. The placement on the cliff gives the swallows an excellent launching place as they take off in a search for food."

"I'd hate to be a baby bird learning how to fly from one of those places," Fannie said. "One mistake, and it's splat!"

"As a matter of fact, some babies don't make it, and sometimes a strong storm will blow some of the nests down the face of the cliff. If you go across the road," Mr. Levin said, "you can find some bird skeletons and the scraps of a few nests."

Fannie made a face. "No thank you," she said. "I think I'll stay here."

"There are several paths up ahead about one hundred feet or so," Mr. Levin said. "They can take you up to the top of the cliff. The paths are safe, and it's a great view. You can even look down and observe some of the birds, since the face of the cliff juts out slightly. Anyone game to go to the top? It will take three-quarters of an hour to hike up and come back. Those who don't want to go can rest here, have a snack, and keep watch over the bikes and gear."

"Count me out," said Dale. "I'm doing better today, but who knows when my muscles will say 'we quit.'"

"I think I'll stay here," said Marilyn.

"I'll stay here, too," said Mitchell. "The view is fine and heights sometimes make me woozy."

"Me too," Tom said.

"It's scary, but I think I'll try it. If I'm not going to be the baby, I'm going to have to do things that look difficult," Fannie declared.

"I'll go, too. I don't think it will be all that bad, Fan," Abby said.

Tracey also wanted to go, and Bill said, "I'm going to do both. Grab me some chow here and then go to the top." He strode over to his knapsack, pulled out two candy bars, and unwrapped one of them. He chewed it for a few seconds and then started jogging furiously in place. "Okay, the sugar has kicked in. I'm ready, coach."

Mr. Levin laughed and shook his head. "You get

the prize for the fastest working metabolism on record. All right, Mr. Energy, follow me."

Mr. Levin led the way. Abby and the three others followed. Finally, they found themselves on a plateau that had paths leading off in many directions. The view was incredible, just as Mr. Levin had promised.

"Look to the east," Tracey said, "You can see the tower of the Congregational church back home."

"Look down, and you can see how clever the swallows have been in building their nests. See how they've used any level place as a base, and then woven material around a few twigs so that it remains solid and firm within the crevice." Mr. Levin pointed to where he wanted the students to look.

Tracey took her eyes from the vista to the east and suddenly stared in the direction that Mr. Levin pointed. She gave a little moan, and then her knees buckled.

"Tracey, are you all right?" Mr. Levin asked as he moved quickly and caught her under the arms.

"Ohh, I guess it was the drop when I looked down too suddenly. My stomach just feels queasy. Maybe if I could sit down for a few minutes?"

"Sure. Let's walk back over to those rocks by the path. You can lie down if you like. I'm sure it will pass," Mr. Levin said with concern in his voice. "But better take it easy for a little while."

Mr. Levin escorted Tracey away from the edge of the cliff, and Fannie tagged along behind. "Are you okay, Tracey?" she asked worriedly.

Abby turned to follow them, but unexpectedly

she felt Bill's hand on her shoulder. "Don't go, Abby," he said. "I'd like to talk, just the two of us."

"Bill, I really don't think we should stay out here . . ."

"But I do," he insisted. "I want to know why you're so cool to me."

"Cool?" she asked, amazed. "I'm not cool. I'm just me. How do you expect me to act? We hardly even know each other."

"I'd like to do something about that," Bill said as he reached out and gently touched Abby's cheek with the back of his hand. "This could turn out to be more than just a school trip to the top of Ram's Head. It could be the start of something very fine, you know. You're a terrific girl. I want you to know that's the way I think of you. We could have some real fun for the rest of the trip."

Abby felt flustered, as well as excited and pleased. Bill Kelsey liked her. He was handsome. She had to admit to herself he was more physically attractive than Buddy. She felt Bill's magnetism. She wasn't married to Buddy, of course, but at the back of her mind she knew that even though they had said they'd date other people, she hadn't expected to meet a Bill Kelsey. She needed time to think about what was going on.

"Bill," she said kindly, "you're really nice, but—"

"Don't give me any buts," he said as he grasped both her arms. "You know that I operate on instinct and impulse, and I expect . . ."

"And I expect that it's time to get back to the

others," Mr. Levin said as he suddenly came up in back of them. He had approached quietly and neither Abby nor Bill had heard him.

Bill dropped Abby's arms immediately and said, "Just a little personal talk, Mr. Levin. We'll finish it up at some other time."

Mr. Levin paused, narrowed his eyes, and said, "I think, Bill, that whatever it was that was going on would be best started and 'finished up' after this trip is over. I don't want any complications while we're on the road. Do you understand? And you, too, Abby?"

"But, Mr. Levin," Abby started to protest.

"No ifs or buts," the teacher interrupted. "Tracey's ready to go down. She and the others are waiting for us over there." He nodded to the start of the descending path. "I think that we had better go now." Mr. Levin turned and walked away.

Abby and Bill followed. As she walked toward the others, Abby began to get angry. Mr. Levin acted as if he knew that something was going on between Bill and her. It seemed as if he had already decided that they had done something wrong. Boy, Abby thought to herself, I always said Mr. Levin was special because he was fair and willing to listen to kids. What if Bill and I do have something to discover between us? What business of his is it? Abby continued to steam as they descended the steep trail that led them to the road below. When they got there, she barely grunted a reply when Marilyn asked how she had liked the view.

"That much, eh?" Marilyn joked as she noticed Abby's mood.

Abby tried to smile but she found it difficult. "It wasn't all that it was cracked up to be," she said tersely.

The group started off on the next leg of the trip. As she pedaled, Abby became more and more annoyed. Mr. Levin, she thought, had no right to tell her what to feel and what to do.

When they stopped for their lunch break, Abby leaned her bike against a tree and retreated from the others. She looked up. Since morning the sky had turned a leaden gray. It suited her mood perfectly.

"Come on and have a sandwich with me," said Marilyn as she approached. "What happened up there to put you down in the dumps, an attack of the killer swallows?"

Abby nodded and accepted Marilyn's invitation, but she refused to go into the details of what was bothering her. "Just a passing blue mood. I'll be fine in a little while."

Just before they all settled down to eat, Mr. Levin announced, "We're making good time. Even with our stop for birdwatching, we're slightly ahead of schedule. I think we can take an extra hour on this break. How does that sound?"

"I think it's great," Dale replied, obviously glad to rest his muscles.

"I don't know, Mr. Levin," said Tom. "Look at the sky."

"It could rain, but I'm almost sure that it will hold off until tonight," Mr. Levin replied.

"Oh, great," Bill said. "Just what I need. No fire and a soggy sleeping bag."

"I hope not," Mr. Levin replied. "Let's not borrow

trouble. Instead, I suggest we all relax now. Then if it does rain, we'll be able to cope. Any objections?"

"None here," Bill agreed.

A moment later Dale came thundering through the underbrush. "Hey, everybody, come and see what I just found," he said with an excited voice. "I was out in the woods just a little way from here and discovered something. It's really worth seeing."

"I'm sure," Tracey said doubtfully, "What is it? An ice cream truck? I was just about to dig into a 'scrumptious' deviled ham handwich. This better be worth it, Dale."

"I don't want to spoil the surprise. Come and see." Dale retreated back into the woods from where he had come, and the others followed.

"There's no path over there," Fannie said. "What was Dale doing out in the middle of the woods?"

"Think about it for a second, Fannie," Marilyn said. "Why do any of us go into the woods off the path all by ourselves?"

Fannie paused. "Oh," she said, and she blushed slightly.

"Let's see what he's found," Tom said. "It might be something exciting."

"It might be something dumb, too," Tracey said, "but we might as well see what it is. If it's a waste of time, Dale will have to carry the stove as a punishment."

"I'm right behind you," said Mr. Levin. "Let's see what Dale has discovered."

The group followed Dale, who was thirty yards ahead of them. When they had walked for only two minutes, he stopped and called, "It's over here I think." He paused. "No, I don't see it. I think I'm a bit mixed up. It's over there to the left. Follow me." Then he lumbered off for another forty yards.

"This had better be good," Marilyn said. "I'm getting hungry, and I sure could go for that rest Mr. Levin promised us."

They walked on and finally came to where Dale was standing. He pointed straight ahead. "Look at that," he said, "pretty interesting, right?"

They all looked to where he was pointing. At first, none of them could see anything unusual.

"Hey, Dale," Tom said, "Are you sure you weren't smoking something funny out here? I think you must be hallucinating."

Then Mr. Levin pointed, too, and said, "Why, that's amazing. I didn't know there were caves around here."

Abby strained her eyes and looked again. Caves? Then she, too, saw it. In front of them, in what at first looked like a large hill, was an opening almost completely covered over with green vines. As they stood there, the breeze ruffled the vines, and they could see the opening more clearly.

"Isn't it great?" Dale said. "At first I didn't notice it either, but then a rabbit hopped by, right in front of me, and sort of disappeared behind the vines. I waited for it to reappear, but it didn't. Finally, I realized that I was staring at that opening."

"A huge rabbit hole," Marilyn said. "Sort of like *Alice in Wonderland*, except bigger."

"Should we go in and explore it?" Dale asked.

"Are you crazy?" Tracey replied. "*Anything* could live in there, and I don't mean little screech owls like the one we heard last night. It could even be the start of an underground tunnel. I've read stories about people getting stuck underground and never getting out. No thanks—I'm not going in there. Let's all go back and eat our lunch."

"How about it, Mr. Levin?" Bill asked, as if he hadn't heard a word that Tracey had said. "It might be kind of fun to find out what it's all about. It might even be an unknown geological phenomenon. We'll get our names in the papers for discovering it."

"I doubt that," Mr. Levin said, "but I have to admit that I'm intrigued. Tell you what. Mitchell, you run back to the campsite and get a couple of flashlights. Bring them back here. I don't think that we can just go off and ignore Dale's discovery."

"But, Mr. Levin . . ." Tracey started to object.

"Tracey, you don't have to go in with the rest of us if you don't want to, but I guarantee that if a rabbit went into the cave the way Dale says it did, nothing fierce lives in there."

"I've got to say that I've always been fascinated by caves," Tom said. "It must be because of all those pirate books I read and loved when I was in the fourth grade. Pirates were always hiding their stolen treasure in caves, then getting ready and killing each other over the gold. Only their skeletons would reamin, slowly turning into dust to remind anyone who stumbled upon them that crime does not pay."

"Skeletons? That does it!" Abby said.

Bill walked up to the mouth of the cave and pulled the curtain of green vines apart. He peered in. "It looks big and dark," he said.

"Brilliant deduction, Sherlock!" Tom said.

"Just hold on a minute, Bill," Mr. Levin commanded. "Mitchell will be back with the lights any second. Then we can all go in."

"Anything you say, Mr. Levin," Bill answered in a bored voice. "Anything you say."

Just then, Mitchell appeared. "Here," he said, handing one of the two flashlights to Mr. Levin.

"Thanks, Mitch," the teacher said. "Now, who's going on this expedition?"

"Wow. Climbing and spelunking all on the same day," Abby said as she held up her hand. "This trip isn't all bad."

All the others except Tracey, raised their hands, too.

"I refuse to be the only one left out, so I guess I'll have to go into the stupid cave," Tracey said. "But I'm running out at the first sign of anything weird. I have too much to live for."

"Let's go," said Mr. Levin. "I'll lead. Mitchell, you get near the end of the line so that we'll have lights fore and aft. Here goes."

Mr. Levin ducked into the cave. One by one, the others followed. They found that they could stand up once they were inside. Mr. Levin shone his flashlight all around what seemed to be a large room with a high ceiling. Abby couldn't see the back wall. She shivered. The temperature inside the cave was considerably lower than outside. While the early spring weather they had been experiencing could not be described as warm, the cave seemed to be a place where winter still lurked.

The flashlight beams searched restlessly around

the cave. The group moved forward slowly. Abby found that her eyes were becoming used to the dark. It wasn't as pitch black inside as she had first thought. She could just about make out the forms of Fannie and Mitchell, who were on each side of her. She was beginning to enjoy the feeling of being on an expedition to a strange and unknown place.

"Look up there," Mitchell said, pointing his flashlight to the ceiling. The light hit several small objects that looked like small stones. Then the stones moved!

"Bats! Those are bats!" Tracey said. "I'm getting out of here. Don't you know that bats have rabies and that they can get stuck in your hair and bite you?"

"Don't be ridiculous, Tracey," Abby heard Mr. Levin say. "Bats have no more interest in you than you have in them. The last case of rabies in this state caused by a bat bite was reported about forty years ago. Just be calm, will you? Bats—they're harmless."

"I think the words *bat* and *harmless* are mutually exclusive," Tracey sniffed, "but if you'll turn out the light you're shining on them, I'll agree not to run out of here screaming."

"Gee, Tracey, I can't tell you how happy that makes me feel," Bill said sarcastically.

"Enough about the bats," said Mr. Levin. "They're not going to hurt you. Now, don't shine your light up there again, please. Let's try to find out now what else is in this cave." He directed his flashlight straight in front of him.

After he had taken several steps ahead, Mr. Levin

said, "Well, I guess we're not the only ones to have found this place. There go your newspaper headlines, Bill."

Abby and the others inched up to where their teacher was standing. As they drew up to him, the beam of Mr. Levin's flashlight picked out the back of the cave. There, painted in large spray-paint letters, were the words, DELTA KAPPA EPSILON LIVES FOREVER!

"So much for our journey into the unknown," Marilyn said, as she observed a pyramid of beer cans piled under the crudely lettered sign, BATS, BEER AND DKE.

"You know, that makes me mad," Tom said. "Why do people have to spoil everything?"

"I know just how you feel, Tom," Mr. Levin said, "but humans have always wanted to make their mark on any place they've been—caves included. I'll show you why. Mitchell, when I say 'three,' put out your light, and keep it out until I say to put it on again."

Before anyone had a chance to protest, Mr. Levin was finished counting: ". . . three." He turned his flashlight off and, after hesitating a few seconds, Mitch did the same.

The cave was plunged into absolute darkness. As she stood in the silent dark, Abby began to feel a tide of panic rising inside her. She felt vulnerable and reached out, anxious to make contact with someone. After what seemed an incredibly long time, she felt a warm hand and clasped it.

"Mr. Levin, please put on the lights," Abby said, trying to hide the panic she felt.

"Yeah, *now,* please," Tom said.

Mr. Levin switched his flashlight on, and Mitchell did the same. "Now you understand that making a mark is man's way of beating back the dark. I think it's a universal sensation to feel alone when the dark closes in."

"You're right, Mr. Levin. The dark is scary," said Tracey. "Can we get out of here now? I've had it with this cave and I'm hungry."

"Yes, Tracey," Mr. Levin answered. "Mitchell, could you lead us back to the entrance?"

"Sure, Mr. Levin," Mitchell said. Still holding Abby's hand lightly, he turned and made his way toward the entrance.

As they emerged from behind the vines Mitchell's hand was touching Abby's, but when Abby saw Bill looking at them, she quickly disengaged her grasp. "Thanks," she said briefly. "I guess I'm never going to lead an expedition to the center of the earth."

"Anytime," Mitchell said.

Mr. Levin emerged from the cave and smiled at Dale. "A round of applause for Dale. The cave might not be a brand-new discovery, but I think we've all learned something."

"All right, everybody back to camp for a hearty lunch!"

Abby fell into line behind Mitchell. As she looked at his slim back, she wondered why she had let go of him suddenly. His hand had felt soft and reassuring. She was surprised at herself that Bill's opinion should influence her. Bill would be nothing more than an unwanted complication on this trip.

She vowed that she would ignore him, in fact, forget about all boys — until the trip was over. Mr. Levin was right. A biking trip over spring vacation was hardly the time to think about starting a new romance. And anyway, there was Buddy. He was special to her. She didn't know if he had someone at college. Sometimes she hated herself for imagining the worst.

When they got back to the campsite, everyone dove into the food, then settled down for a short after-lunch siesta. Mr. Levin stretched out on a nearby slab of rock. Mitchell began to tinker with the brakes on his bike. Abby felt obliged to explain her behavior in the cave.

"Thanks for giving me a helping hand," she said.

"No problem. I guess I held on a little too long though," he said, looking at the brake gears.

"Don't be silly," Abby said. "It was good to have something to hold onto."

"And I just happened to be there, right?" Mitchell replied. "I think that someone else is waiting to talk to you right now." He turned back to his bike.

Abby looked over her shoulder. Bill was approaching. "If you can spare me a minute, I think that we have some unfinished business," he said calmly.

Abby thought of the vow she had made as she walked back from the cave. "Bill," she said quietly, "I don't know what exactly was happening up there on the cliffs, but I think that maybe the best thing to do is to cool it. I'm mad at Mr. Levin for jumping to conclusions, but, on the other hand, he was right about some things. Let's make a truce. No hard feelings."

Bill looked at her with such sincerity that she found all her resolve melting away. "I'd like to remedy the fact that you think I was just flirting for kicks." Bill smiled again and gave her a wink. Then he motioned for her to follow him. He left the group and disappeared down one of the small trails that led to another clearing.

Abby knew that she could stay where she was or she could be adventurous and go against Mr. Levin's advice. Standing in the middle of the clearing, Abby knew she had a choice. She didn't need Bill Kelsey, but she didn't want to seem immature and cowardly. She glanced quickly back toward Mr. Levin. He seemed thoroughly engrossed in his reading. Abby took a deep breath and followed Bill.

She saw him leaning against a tree. The breeze ruffled his hair, and he had pulled his collar up to ward off the chill. Abby couldn't help noticing how appealing he looked.

"'Thought you weren't coming," he said casually.

"I don't know whether I should have or not," Abby replied.

"Oh, yes you do. That's why you came."

"You're pretty confident," Abby said.

"No," Bill replied. "I just think there might be something special between us. The chemistry feels right."

"We don't even know each other."

"We can fix that right now," he said as he reached for her.

Abby felt his strong arms around her, then suddenly, as if he changed his mind, Bill released her and took a step backward.

"Bill . . ." Abby began, but she didn't finish the sentence. Mr. Levin was standing behind them.

"I thought that I told you just a couple of hours ago to cool it. Abby, I have to say that I'm surprised and a little disappointed in you. As for you, Bill, I chalked up the incident with the shopping cart as an "accident." I didn't want to start up but I still can't believe only Abby was to blame. But I've had it now. I want you to stop. There is no going off alone. I don't want to spend any time worrying about whether or not you two are staying with the group."

"Mr. Levin," Abby said, "I think you've misinterpreted this. We're not doing anything wrong."

"Abby," Mr. Levin said, "what you do on your own time is your own business, but this trip belongs to all the kids who have elected to come along. I won't, repeat, won't, have the group's activities thrown off by two people who are choosing to act inappropriately."

"Mr. Levin," Bill said. "We get the point. There was nothing serious going on here. Now I understand. Abby understands. We're sorry if you're angry. We didn't think we were doing anything wrong. Let's go back and join the others."

With that, Bill passed in front of her and started up the path, but as he brushed past, he quickly squeezed her hand.

Abby felt confused and humiliated. As she headed back she passed Mr. Levin, and she said quietly,

"I'm sorry, Mr. Levin, I wasn't thinking about the others. I acted foolishly."

"Abby," Mr. Levin said calmly, "just don't let this happen again. I certainly didn't expect this from you. I thought I could trust you completely."

Abby returned to the group and managed to avoid the curious eyes that fastened upon her. She thought of her Zodiac friends who were probably having a fabulous time together. She thought of Buddy. Her misery increased until Mr. Levin called, "Rest period is over. Let's get going." Abby struggled to put on her backpack and was surprised when Mitchell came over and helped her.

"Ready to go?" he asked. "Whatever's wrong will get better, I guarantee it."

"Who says?" Abby answered. She looked at him and rolled her eyes. This guy is too nice, she thought to herself, or I'm still in a bad mood.

The group remounted their bikes and began the afternoon ride. The weather seemed to change to match Abby's mood. The sun disappeared behind a fine veil of clouds, and the sky looked as if it had been bruised. Large, dark clouds made Abby feel as if she were riding at early evening. Then a brisk, cold wind sprang up. The band of cyclists put their heads down and pedaled hard to make headway. After a half-hour of hard riding, a cold drizzle began to slick the countryside. Mr. Levin called for a halt.

"This isn't any fun," said Fannie as she dismounted.

"It's a challenge, Fannie," Mr. Levin replied. "We were ahead of schedule—that's why I gave you the rest period this afternoon, but I should have listened to Tom and had us push on. This weather is worse than I anticipated. I made a mistake."

Abby thought Mr. Levin looked at her while he made his comments, but she quickly told herself that she was being paranoid. Mr. Levin might be angry with her, but he'd never embarrass her in front of the others. You're feeling miserable enough without finding more reasons to be depressed, she told herself.

"What we're going to do," Mr. Levin said, "is put on our rain gear and keep going. There's a public campground up ahead with lean-tos where we can spend the night and use our stove. Aren't you glad we brought it along, Tracey?" he asked, trying to regain some spirit. "Doesn't it make carrying it this afternoon just a little less of a pain?"

"I'm not sure," Tracey said glumly. "It throws my center of balance way off. I wish we could have sent it ahead by taxi!"

Mr. Levin continued, "This campground is about ten miles from Ram's Head. Once we start up the road to the top of the mountain, it really isn't a difficult ride."

"But, Mr. Levin," Dale complained as they pulled out their ponchos, "why not stop here and try to wait out the storm? I don't see myself as Hillary scaling Everest. If we don't get to Ram's Head on time, or ever get there at all for that matter, so what?"

"I agree," Tracey added. "Enough's enough."

The thought of not making it to Ram's Head in time for the solstice filled Abby with such disappointment that she snapped angrily, "Oh, come on, Tracey. We'll just get more cold and miserable by the minute waiting here. If we're cycling, we'll keep warm and get someplace."

"I know the thought of not being on that mountain for your Aries solstice makes you cry, O Queen of the Druids," Tracey shot back, matching Abby's sharp tone with one of her own, "but I am perfectly warm right here."

Tom and Mitchell raised their hands in a gesture of peace. Tom said, "Stop bickering please. I think that the weather is getting to us all."

"You both have a point, Tracey," Mitchell added. "But what if the weather doesn't break? We'd be stuck here on the side of the road for the night. The thought of spending the night in a lean-to, while not the same as staying at the Ritz, does seem a lot more attractive than the possibility of spending it here."

"Right," said Mr. Levin. "As long as the wind and the rain don't get much worse, we're going to keep going. I think we can reach the campground in about two hours."

"Really?" asked Marilyn. "That will get us there by dinner. That's not too bad."

"We can build a fire," Mr. Levin continued, "dry out and relax. I think you can make it, Tracey, and so can the rest of you. I'll take the lead and set the pace. Slow and steady wins the race."

"Good advice for turtles," Bill said. "Too bad I left my shell at home." Then he mounted his bike.

"I didn't bargin for this," Dale mumbled.

As the others mounted their bikes, Abby overheard Dale talking to Tracey. "I have to agree with you, Tracey, but the queen bee had to shoot off her mouth and of course, her drone agreed. There's nothing we can do about it, I guess. I had better save my breath for the 'fun ride ahead." He hoisted his girth onto his bike and set out along the road.

Abby rode behind Dale. How dare he think that I am the queen bee around here, she thought, but she decided that there would be no point in confronting Dale.

Mr. Levin set an easy pace. Despite the rain, Abby did not find the going difficult. Instead, she found herself thinking and rethinking everything that had happened. She remembered the mixed feelings with which she had begun the ride. She had had some misgivings about the group, but wanted to believe that most of them would be really fine. Marilyn was nice, and Fannie was just young and insecure. She would grow up and leave her giggles behind. Tracey was a complainer, but since they were keeping away from each other, she could be tolerated. As for the boys, Tom wasn't really worth discussing. Dale was the kind of person that Abby couldn't understand and generally didn't like. He was not only out of shape, but was too soft on himself. Of course, what he said around the campfire made Abby understand Dale a bit better, but understanding, she realized, did not necessarily translate into "liking."

Her thoughts turned to Mitch and Bill. Mitchell had turned out to be different from what she first thought. He seemed to be more mature than the others on the trip, yet somehow he was so quiet he seemed to lack spontaneity and fun. Oh no, Abby thought, I'm always more interested in bad boys! If Mr. Levin could be thought of as the teacher, Mitchell seemed like the counselor-in-training. Abby thought of her own experience at Spruce Hill Camp last summer as a CIT. Mitchell had all the right qualities. Trying to think of a more concrete image of Mitchell, Abby couldn't help but compare him to one of her favorite actors: Jimmy Stewart! He was not really handsome, but he had sensitivity and brains that set him apart from the others. In fact, he was something like Buddy. But Buddy was in college, and he had more going for him than Mitchell. Yet she couldn't shake the feeling that Mitchell was someone she could probably really talk to and enjoy.

As for Bill, he was exciting. Abby had to confess she found him handsome, and he gave off an aura of being on top of things. There was something about him that was hidden, mysterious, and just a bit dangerous. The possibility that he was attracted to her was appealing. Yet, thinking about the scene earlier in the afternoon made Abby's stomach tighten.

"Darn it," she said as she rode through a puddle, "I wonder what the other Zodiacs would think of all of this." She wondered what they were doing at Penny's. "They certainly can't be as wet and confused as I am," she said under her breath as she grimly pedaled on. "I wish I had Cathy or J.L. to talk to," she mused.

As if some force from Ram's Head Mountain heard the wishes of the cyclists through the sodden countryside, the rain stopped and the wind dropped.

"Hurray!" yelled Fannie excitedly. The others echoed her relief and enthusiasm for the change of atmosphere.

Marilyn drew abreast of Abby and said, "Smile! You've been frowning since after lunch. The clouds are breaking. Things are looking up."

Abby glanced in Marilyn's direction and tried to give her a smile. It was true. She had been acting like a thundercloud for long enough, but the smile felt more like a grimace on her lips.

"That's better," Marilyn said. "I'm a good listener if you need to talk."

They approached a steep incline and, as she leaned into the work of pedaling hard, Abby said, "Thanks, Marilyn. I think I can handle it, but I mean it, thanks." Then Abby lowered her head, hunched her shoulders, and ended the conversation by speeding ahead. She hoped Mr. Levin would try to pick up the pace while the weather held. She really wanted to get to the campground early. Seeing the sunrise on the morning of the vernal equinox would restore her Aries optimism and determination. Once she had experienced this event, she felt certain the trip home would soothe her confusion. She would try to right things with Mr. Levin; she would even try to enjoy everyone's company. First, however, she had to get to Ram's Head. Somehow she felt many of the things troubling her would clear up once she had attained her goal—reaching the peak at her birth sign's natural rebirth.

"Don't despair!" Mr. Levin shouted back over his shoulder as the clouds became dark once again. "I'm sure we're halfway there. We only have about five more miles to go!"

They slogged along as the rain grew heavier. Abby was glad to have a good poncho. Without it, she knew that she would have been miserably cold and wet. She narrowed her eyes and peered ahead through the gloom. The dark sky deepened another shade as the day began to come to an end. It would be good to get off her bike and into a dry lean-to. She looked up to see how the others were faring. If she hated this ride, it probably was agony for Dale.

It was obvious that the dark rain and the effort of the ride were catching up with Dale. Abby noticed his bike wobbling under him. The distance between him and Tom, who preceded him in line, seemed to be growing.

Abby decided to try to be nice to the pudgy, uncoordinated boy in front of her. I'm not a queen bee, but maybe I haven't been too nice to him, she thought. "Keep going, Dale!" she yelled out in an effort to encourage him. "You're doing fine!"

Dale turned his head to try to hear Abby's call, but as he twisted his body and peered back over his left shoulder, disaster struck.

What looked like an innocent puddle turned out to be a huge rut. The riders that preceded him had negotiated it successfully, but Dale, not paying strict attention to where he was going, rode directly into it.

As if it had a life of it's own, Dale's bike leaped out of control. The handle bars twisted violently and turned ninety degrees. The bike's forward motion was stopped—its rear wheel flew into the air. Dale bellowed once and went flying forward. He landed heavily with one leg twisted under him.

At first he lay in a heap in the road, a soaked, despondent blob, but after a few seconds he began to howl in pain. "My ankle! Oh, oh, oh, my ankle! I broke my ankle!"

Abby swerved to avoid colliding with Dale or his bike, and then she stopped quickly. She ran to help Dale.

"Dale, don't move. Try to stay still," she yelled, "until we can see how bad it is."

Dale leaned back and continued to groan.

Mr. Levin had ridden several yards before he realized what had happened. He circled back quickly, dropped his bike at the edge of the road, and came running toward them. "What's going on? What happened?" he demanded.

"He hit something in the road. Is he going to be all right?" Abby said.

Mr. Levin approached the boy crouched in the road. "Don't try to move, Dale," he said, "until we check you out."

Dale looked up at the teacher. "Please, please," he said with a little groan, "don't bother to tell me not to move. I *can't* move! Don't you see that?"

Tom pushed forward. "I don't know if it will do

any good, Mr. Levin, but I've had some Red Cross first-aid training."

Mr. Levin nodded at him and said, "Everyone move back. Tom and I will look at Dale. Everything is going to be fine. Just move back out of the way, please. Now, please."

The others moved back and stood by disconsolately in the rain while Mr. Levin and Tom gently eased Dale onto his back and examined his leg. After a few minutes, Mr. Levin got up and walked over to the group. "It doesn't seem like a break," he announced. "But it looks as if he might have sprained it pretty badly."

"Oh, Mr. Levin, what are we going to do?" Fannie said with a sob in her voice. "It's raining, and I'm getting so cold."

"Take it easy, Fannie," Mr. Levin answered. "I've got a plan. It's only half a mile to the campsite. I want you girls to ride on ahead. Marilyn, you make sure Fannie is all right. Tracey, do you think you could manage to haul Dale's backpack the half mile?"

"Great," Tracey muttered. "He falls off the bike and I end up feeling the pain."

"Abby, you'll see the sign, State Campground Sunrise, or Sunset, or something like that. The sign is always out and visible from the road. You lead. Take the path to the left. That will bring you to the lean-tos. See if you can find dry wood. You should be able to; it hasn't been raining all that long. Build a fire if you can. This rain may be a problem, but a roaring fire will feel mighty good. Take out the chill."

"What are you going to do, Mr. Levin?" Tracey asked.

"It's only half a mile to the camp. The boys and I can take turns making a sling with our arms, two of us at a time, and in that way, we can carry Dale there. I doubt that we'll see a car along this route, but if we do, we'll ask for help. If worse comes to worst, we can carry him piggy-back."

"Oh, swell," Bill muttered.

"I want all of us to get to a place for the night. There are no phones around here for miles, so we won't be able to call for help until at least tomorrow morning. If I have to, I can go back down the road several miles to where I saw a turnoff to Allenville. It's one of the few small towns around here. If Dale can't manage to travel in the morning, I'll ride back there and get help. Now take off, and be careful. It's getting dark, and I want you to get off the road as soon as you can. We'll be there soon."

The girls got on their bikes. With Abby in the lead and Marilyn at the rear, they made their way up the road to the sign Mr. Levin had told them about.

They turned in, followed the path, and finally found the lean-tos. They sat down, exhausted by the travel and the events of the day.

"Let's rest for a few minutes," Marilyn said, "then we can start to look for wood. They won't be here so soon. I just don't feel like I can do another thing. What rotten luck."

"The rotten luck was having blubber-butt along in the first place," Tracey said in an annoyed tone.

"My back is killing me from hauling his stuff. We'll never get to the top of the mountain now, or even get to finish the trip, thanks to Dale's wonderful coordination. We'll all have to be rescued or something."

"Hey, you're being a little rough on the poor guy, aren't you?" Marilyn asked. "It wasn't his fault, you know. Freak accidents happen."

Tracey shrugged, "Yeah, to freaks," she muttered under her breath. Then she turned away and unrolled her sleeping bag.

Abby sat quietly and took in the full impact of what Tracey had said. "Rescued . . . never get to the top of the mountain."

It can't be, Abby thought. Dale will be all right. We'll just let him rest here for the day while we all go to the top. That's it. That's how it will work out, she decided. As if to reinforce the optimism of her thought, Abby decided not to sit and brood. Things were going to work out. There was work to be done.

"Everybody," she called, "Mr. Levin asked us to get some wood. Let's see if we can find some dry pieces under the bushes. A fire would feel great to me, and I bet you want one, too."

"Your energy astounds me. Maybe that's what these high-school boys see in you," Tracey said as she slowly got to her feet, "but in this case I welcome it. Point me in the right direction, put the flashlight in my hand so I won't kill myself in the dark, and let's go."

"Please, can we stay together," Fannie pleaded.

"Deserted campgrounds make me think of crazies on the loose."

"Any crazy person would have to be *crazy* to be out in this weather," Marilyn said. "But you're right, Fannie, it's best if we stick together."

As the four girls set out, the rain became a drizzle, then stopped entirely. They looked under bushes and shrubs for dry pieces of wood. Before they had gone too far, Tracey pointed and said. "Do you see what I see?" Ahead of them was an arrow-shaped sign that said WOOD.

"Looks like we could be in luck," Abby said. "These measly little pieces that we found will burn up in a minute."

They followed the sign. Before long they found a shed that was half-filled with both big and little logs.

"Thank you, Mr. Forest Ranger, or Smoky the Bear, or whoever chopped down all this beautiful wood and left it for us poor, wet cyclists," Tracey said. "Come on, Fannie, help me load up." She extended her arms in front of her. "If we each take four or five pieces, we'll have a great bonfire before the guys arrive."

When the others limped into the camp a half-hour later, the two groups each had a surprise for the other. The boys were astounded to see the fire, and the girls were amazed to see that Dale, although limping badly, actually walked into the camp.

"Dale, you're better. How terrific," Marilyn said.

Mr. Levin replied, "Well, he's not going to go on a major hike by himself, but once we had carried him three quarters of the way, Dale thought he could negotiate the rest."

"And I did," Dale said proudly.

"A true example of the walking wounded," Bill added.

"We even managed to bring all of the bikes with us," Tom said with a smile, "so once Dale has a chance to eat and rest his leg overnight, we can all take off in the morning, right?"

"Right, I guess," Dale answered somewhat doubtfully. "Thanks for bringing my gear, Tracey."

"You're welcome," she said in an overly polite tone.

Hearing Tom's words, Abby felt that her earlier optimism had not been misplaced. Everything was going to work out after all. Dale hadn't hurt himself all that badly—they would be off to Ram's Head early in the morning. It wasn't that far. Surely Dale would be able to make it or take care of himself here in the camp until they returned.

Mr. Levin put up his hand. "Let's see how things go with Dale's leg before we start making any plans. He's taken a nasty spill. Just because he's limped one hundred yards doesn't mean that he'll be ready to ride his bike tomorrow."

Abby's spirits sank a little as she listened, but she refused to believe there was a chance that she was not going to ride to the top of the mountain tomorrow. She told herself that Mr. Levin, like all adults, tended to be too conservative in estimating any situation.

The storm seemed to be over for good. While they prepared a supper of soup and omelets made with powdered eggs, Abby looked up and saw a star twinkle briefly. Dale declared himself too stiff to walk another step, and obviously enjoyed sitting in the lean-to and shouting orders to the others. Humoring the resident invalid, they did his bidding with only occasional complaints. Things did seem to be getting better. Finally, it was time to eat. Everyone reached for the plates, eager to begin.

Abby felt that Bill deliberately took a seat away from her. Soon he appeared to be deep in a conversation with Tom and Mr. Levin. Abby told herself it was best that they didn't seem to be pairing off. Mr. Levin wouldn't like it, and besides, did she even want to be with Bill? She turned to her right and discovered Mitchell had come to sit beside her.

"Some day, huh?" he asked as he sipped his soup.

"I've had better," Abby replied.

"Me too, but I guess I look on it as something we'll all talk about for a long time. I think some good has come out of the whole experience."

"Clue me in," Abby said. "What good do you see in riding through the rain and having our plans almost spoiled by an unforeseen accident?"

"Oh, I didn't mean today, really," Mitchell answered. "But we can cope, and that's something."

Abby wrinkled her nose in doubt. Mitchell continued, "What I meant is that the trip has given us all a chance to widen our circles. You know, high school is such a fragmented place, and people get known by reputations whether they deserve them or not. I mean, look at you, for instance."

"Me?" Abby said, feeling slightly flustered. "Do I have a reputation I don't deserve?"

"A lot of kids say that you're kind of conceited and want to have everything your own way," he said.

"Now wait a second," Abby said earnestly, "that's not fair, I . . ."

Mitch gave her a big smile. "Now I know it isn't true, but I never would have known how terrific you are if we hadn't been on this trip together. He stretched and then looked at her directly. "And what did you think about me before the trip? The truth, now."

Abby felt the heat rush to her face. It was more than just the warmth from the fire that was making her feel flushed. "Well," she began, "reports were kind of mixed."

Mitch laughed. "Computer nerd, mixed with what? Mad scientist? Grind?"

"No, no," Abby started to protest, and then she laughed in return. "Well, a bit of a computer nerd, but a friend of mine said you were nice."

"That's secondhand. But who said it, anyway? What do you think now that you have firsthand information?"

Abby, who prided herself on being direct, hesitated a moment. She looked at Mitchell's honest, open face and felt a surge of affection for him. It wasn't what she felt when she noticed Bill, but it made her feel relaxed and happy. "My friend was right," she said, "you are nice. My friend is Mara Bennett."

"See," said Mitch in a low, gentle voice. "I told you some good had come out of this trip. Abby . . ."

Before he could go any further, Mr. Levin called him. "I'd like you to help me here."

"Sure, Mr. Levin," Mitchell replied. Before he left her side, he said, "Good talking, Abby, really." Then he went over to Mr. Levin.

"What was that all about?" Tracey asked with a slight sneer in her voice. "Are you going to try to set some sort of a record for most boys won over on a camping trip?"

"Not all the boys, Tracey," Abby said cheerfully. "You can have Tom and Dale." Then Abby got up and moved toward the fire.

Mr. Levin got up from where he had been crouching and walked to the center of the campsite. "Can I have your attention, please?" he asked. "I've got some disappointing news. Dale's ankle has really puffed up. I'm awfully sorry, but I don't think we can go any farther. The trip to Ram's Head in the morning is off. I'll go back to Allenville and get a vehicle up here to drive Dale back home. Perhaps after that's arranged, and I've phoned Dale's parents, we can continue. But I can't promise anything. We'll have to see how the day goes tomorrow. I know how much some of you were counting on being there early tomorrow. But this is the verdict."

"Hey, Mr. Levin, why can't we go on up to the peak while you take care of Dale?" Bill asked.

"I'm afraid not, Bill. You can't go riding without supervision. I took the responsibility for your safety when you signed up for the trip, and I just won't have you riding alone."

"But we're not babies," Fannie protested.

"I know that, Fannie," said Mr. Levin. "You probably could ride from here to Timbuktu without anything going wrong, but there's no way we can risk it."

Abby felt her mood roller-coaster from the contentment she had been feeling to disappointment and then to anger. They were so close to their destination. She was so close to making her fantasy a reality. Fannie was right. They weren't babies. Mr. Levin said he was sorry, but he obviously didn't know how much it meant.

"It isn't fair!" she said in a loud voice. "We've just got to go on, Mr. Levin. We were counting on it. It's very important. We've got to go. One person can't be allowed to spoil it for the rest of us!"

Dale looked up, "Don't blame me, Queen Abby. None of this would have happened if you hadn't yelled at me and taken my attention off the road. If it's anyone's fault, it's yours!"

"It was an accident, Dale, and nobody's blaming anybody. Abby, I know that it may not seem fair, but I've made my decision, and I'm the one in charge. Now the discussion is ended, and I don't want to hear any more about it. All right?" Mr. Levin finished.

Abby opened her mouth to protest again, but the look in Mr. Levin's eyes stopped her. She turned her back and walked into the flickering shadows cast by the fire. You are not going to cry, she told herself. You are not going to cry. But she wanted to more than anything else in the world.

Each member of the group went solitarily about his business. Tom unrolled his sleeping bag to get ready for the night. Fannie dug into her backpack, found some marshmallows, and began toasting them without offering any to anyone else. Marilyn crouched in front of the fire and seemed self-absorbed. Dale sat on his bedroll with a scowl on his face, as if waiting for someone to accuse him of spoiling everyone's good time. Mr. Levin and Tracey rearranged the tarpaulin over the supply of wood.

Mitchell slowly walked to the edge of the campsite toward Abby. Seeing him coming, she shook her head no. She couldn't face the idea of talking to anyone. From where he was standing, Bill watched Mitchell approach Abby and saw her refusal. He smiled slightly, and then he moved closer to the fire and stretched, enjoying the comfort of the heat it provided.

The silence was not the comfortable kind that can come about after a long, satisfying day. Instead it seemed to weigh on everybody like a sodden pall. Finally, Tom spoke up. "Well," he said, "since we've had so much fun so far this evening, who'd like to join me in a game of Botticelli?"

"Too hard and *too* pretentious," Tracey said.

"Geography?" Tom asked.

"Too easy," Fannie replied.

"Twenty questions?"

"Too dumb," Marilyn sighed.

His voice rising to a piteous squeak, Tom asked again, "Telephone?"

Mitchell laughed and said, "That might lighten things up around here. Why not? Want to join us, Abby?" he added, trying to make his voice as non-committal as possible.

Abby, still upset, but not wanting to act like a spoiled child, gave a shrug and joined the group that was forming around the fire.

"How do you play?" Fannie asked.

"What? You've never played telephone?" Bill asked in mock surprise. "How did you get through elementary school?"

"*Poor* child," Marilyn said, adopting Bill's tone, "a perfect example of a deprived childhood."

"Okay, you guys," Fannie answered, obviously pleased to be the center of attention. "Cut the fooling and just tell me how to play, will you?"

"It's simple, Fannie," said Mr. Levin. "A person thinks of a one-sentence message, then whispers it to the person next to him. That person whispers it to the next person and so on until the last person announces what he's heard. Then the head of the line goes to the end, everyone moves up a place, and a new message starts on its way. It's cheating to change the message deliberately—you have to whisper exactly what you heard."

Dale, who was still sitting in the lean-to, said, "Let me play will you? Someone help me over there."

Mr. Levin went to help Dale move to the fire, and the others settled down in a row. "I'm all set," Dale said when he arrived in the middle of the group. "Who goes first?"

"I'm first in line," Tracey said. "I'll give the first message." The whole group was caught up in enthusiasm for the silly children's game that they would have scorned as too juvenile at almost any other time. Abby found herself between Bill and Fannie.

"Do you have the feeling this is ridiculous?" Bill said.

"Yes, now shut up and start whispering," Fannie replied.

Tracey smiled as she began her message: *William Shakespeare wrote* The Taming of the Shrew *with a quill pen.* When it was finally announced as "Will shaped the spear and wrote time into screw neath a quilted pin," everyone laughed. All the others came out equally ridiculous. No one mentioned that they would not be cycling to Ram's Head Mountain in the morning.

Finally, Mr. Levin announced, "One more and then I'm going to hit the sack. Fannie, you start the message, and Abby, since you're last in line, you announce it."

Fannie thought about her message for a long time.

"Please don't whisper the Gettysburg Address," Tom said. "It doesn't have to be long to be good."

"I've got it," Fannie said. "It's a good one." She leaned over to Mr. Levin and started.

After the message got to Bill, Abby cocked her head, ready to receive it. "I want to talk to you after everyone's asleep," Bill whispered. "Stay awake. I'll come and get you."

"What," said Abby, at first not understanding what Bill had said.

"No fair repeating," Fannie said. "Just blurt it out, Abby."

"The message is—the message is—" Abby hesitated and Bill looked at her and winked.

"The figs in the garden of the ogre smell like Tony's toes," Abby said, trying to make it sound as if someone really got confused.

"What?" Fannie demanded. "Someone must have loused my message up on purpose. That doesn't come close. What I said was, 'The sun also rises on the day after the solstice.' That was supposed to cheer you up, Abby."

"Sorry, Fannie. That's what I thought Bill said," Abby replied. "Anyway, your message really wouldn't do what you wanted it to do."

"Games like this can go on only so long before my old brain starts to turn to mush," Mr. Levin said. "Good-night, all."

"'Night, Mr. Levin." Bill said in a loud voice, and then he added quietly, "So, Abby?"

"We'll see," Abby answered and turned and walked to the lean-to where the girls were spending the night. She wondered what Bill could possibly want to talk to her about when everyone else was asleep.

And wouldn't you be stupid to get up and talk to him, she told herself. You're already in enough hot water with Mr. Levin without doing something you know he'd disapprove of. No way.

Nonetheless, as she unrolled her sleeping bag and took some water from her canteen to brush her teeth, Abby couldn't stop herself from imagining a meeting with Bill. It wasn't for the romance. It was more for the adventure. She hated to go home and tell the Zodiacs that her trip had been a big zero. But the only sensible thing to do was to crawl into her sleeping bag and try to sleep until the morning. Glad to have made such a reasonable decision, Abby said good-night to the other girls and closed her eyes.

Abby awoke suddenly and let out a gasp. Someone had poked her in the back and was whispering her name. Fogged by sleep, she momentarily forgot where she was. Then she turned over and saw a dark silhouette standing by the edge of the lean-to. She realized that Bill, true to his word, had come to pick her up. He held a long stick that he had obviously used to prod her, and he whispered, "Easy, Abby. It's only me."

"You're crazy. Go away," she said groggily. She rolled over and put her head down.

She felt the stick prod her again. "I told you I wanted to talk to you," Bill said. "Everybody else is asleep. Let's . . ."

"Go back to bed," Abby whispered urgently. She looked at her watch. Its luminous dial told her that it was four o'clock. "We're not getting up for another two hours," she said, and she pulled her sleeping bag up over her head.

For the third time the stick pushed into her back. "Abby, please. It can't wait."

Tracey turned in her sleep and groaned. Swell, Abby thought, all I need is for Tracey to wake up and see Bill trying to lure me away from the lean-to. She'll tell the whole school the story. Why does Bill live dangerously, unlike everyday, normal boys?

With a sigh of annoyance, Abby carefully extricated herself from her sleeping bag, tiptoed over the sleeping forms that surrounded her, and joined Bill at the edge of the lean-to. "I'm only doing this so the others don't wake up. Now, what is it you want?" Abby asked.

"Please, not so loud," Bill whispered. "Come over by the fire." He took her hand and led her away from the lean-to.

They stood next to the few glowing embers. Bill murmured, "It's almost time."

"Almost time for what?" Abby asked.

"To split—to see the sun rise from the top of Ram's Head."

"Are you crazy?" Abby asked. "You heard what Mr. Levin said."

"I thought seeing the sun rise from the top of Ram's Head was really important to you. It's the reason you came on this trip. At least that's what you said."

Abby nodded her agreement.

"Well, then, let's go. I want to be with the Zodiac

Queen as she stands brave against the sky."

Bill reached out to touch her, but Abby took a step back and said, "No, Bill. You're making fun of me." Nonetheless, his words excited something restless in her. She tried to retain her composure, then said, "Anway, we'd be breaking the rules."

"Rules?" he asked incredulously. "The rules don't count when they're stupid. Mr. Levin can treat the others like babies if he wants, but he's not going to make a baby out of me. Is he going to make you into one? Is this a joke to you, after all?"

"Keep your voice down. Do you want to wake everybody? I don't want to be a baby, but Mr. Levin trusts us," Abby declared.

Bill snorted. "He doesn't trust us. Otherwise, he would have agreed to let us go on without him."

Abby had to agree that Bill was right. Despite herself, she became intrigued with the idea of slipping away to Ram's Head. If they left right away, they'd be back only a little while after the others had awakened. Still, the thought of the trouble they would be in when Mr. Levin found them gone deterred her.

"But Bill, it's so dark. We wouldn't be able to see the road."

For an answer, Bill pointed to the sky. The pitch black of the night before had given way to a lighter shade. Abby sensed that before long the sky would be turning gray as it prepared to usher in the coming dawn. The day of the equinox would be beautiful. Should she dare? Abby trembled slightly, and her teeth chattered.

"You're cold," Bill said. He reached for her, and this time she did not back away. "What do you say, Aries," he asked as his strong arms surrounded her.

"I don't know, I . . ."

Bill dropped his arms. "I thought you were determined to go to the top," he whispered fiercely, "but I guess I was wrong. Well, go back to your sleeping bag, Abby, and give my regards to Mr. Levin in the morning. I'm going whether you are or not." He turned and strode away, took a few steps, and then turned back to her. "I'll tell you what it it was like at breakfast—maybe."

Abby stood rooted to the spot. She felt the way she did when as a child she played games with the other kids on the block. "Red Rover, Red Rover, dare you to come over," they would chant at each other from across an imaginary line. Abby had always been the first to cross the line. Now she took a deep breath and crossed over again.

"Bill, wait!" she said and she hurried to catch up with him. "I'll go."

Bill looked at her and smiled. "I knew you would. I knew you weren't afraid to do your own thing." He held out his hand to her. "Let's go. We don't have much time."

"One thing, though," Abby said, "we've really got to leave Mr. Levin a note. He'll be furious with us, but I don't want him to worry. If we tell him where we are, he'll be less anxious."

Bill frowned. "He'll know where we've gone if he's got any brains. This isn't a class or an exam. It's voluntary. It doesn't count. What can he do?"

"No, I mean it, Bill," Abby said.

"I don't even have any paper. How are we going to leave a note?" Bill asked.

"I have some," Abby said, "in the mini pack attached to my bike's seat. I even have a pencil." She walked over to the place under the trees where the bikes were parked. "Here, wait a second." She dug into the pouch and came up with a small notebook and pencil: *"Mr. Levin, don't be angry with us. The trip to the mountaintop was too important to miss. Will be back by 9:00. Please don't worry. Try to understand. Thanks. Abby and Bill."*

"Finished?" Bill asked.

"Yes," Abby answered. "I think the note is important."

"Fine," Bill said. "Here, give it to me. I'll take it back to the boys' lean-to where Mr. Levin will find it as soon as he wakes up. You get ready. I'll be right back."

Abby handed him the note. She was tempted to go back to her sleeping bag but decided getting to the top of Ram's Head was worth taking this chance. She strapped on her helmet and straightened her bike. She was ready to go.

Bill walked toward the lean-to. When he had gone about halfway, he turned and looked over his shoulder. When he no longer could see Abby, he stopped and slowly counted to ten. Then he took the note, folded it, and slipped it into his shirt pocket. Smiling, he turned and walked quickly back to where Abby was waiting.

"Everything all right?" she asked.

"Fine," he replied. "Couldn't be better. Ready?"

"Ready," she answered excitedly.

"Then, Aries the Ram, let's go and see the sun rise." He hopped on his bike and slowly he pedaled alongside Abby back toward the main road.

8

The highway stretched before them like a ghostly vision. The moon hung low in the horizon. The wind rustled through the pines that bordered the road and sighed like mourners at a funeral. Abby shivered, but couldn't shake some vague feeling she couldn't identify. She was determined to reach the goal of the trip. How could she face herself, her Zodiac friends, or Buddy, if she didn't reach Ram's Head. Abby pushed down on the pedals and, following Bill, began the journey.

At first she had trouble seeing the way in front of her. The details of the road that her eyes observed when she was riding during the day now were indistinct and threatening. She decided the safest thing to do was to ride in the middle of the pavement. Surely no cars would suddenly appear at this time of the morning. In the unlikely case that a car or truck was on the road, its headlights would warn her to pull over to the side long before the vehicle reached her. She certainly didn't want an unseen pothole to cause her the same kind of accident as Dale's, so she stayed away from the side of the road.

Eventually her eyes became used to the light. She called out to Bill, "You can pick up the pace if you want." He nodded, and soon they were riding at a reasonable clip. The sound of the chains revolving on their bikes, the wind in the trees, and their own breathing were the only noises that pierced the stillness of the early morning.

As they pedaled along, Abby couldn't help but think of the sleeping people they had left behind. What were they going to say and think when they woke to discover that she and Bill were gone? Briefly she wondered if she should stop and go back. Abby had never done anything so daring in her life. She had always found ways within the system to accomplish things that had seemed important. Now she was directly disobeying a teacher whom she liked and respected. What had happened to her on this trip, she wondered.

Abby looked up and saw the broad back of the rider in front of her. Was Bill responsible for making her so rebellious? No, she couldn't blame him. She was somewhat surprised by her own behavior and her mind soared in confusion as she cycled along. She just wanted her fantasy to come true and Bill would help make it happen.

They had gone about a mile when Bill looked back over his shoulder. "Why so quiet?" he asked.

"We're biking, Bill. I don't have a lot of extra wind." Abby answered. "Besides, we're out here in the almost dark. It doesn't seem right somehow to chatter like we were riding along at high noon."

"What?" he asked. "That makes no sense at all. Do you think goblins and gremlins will hear you if you make any noise and then come out of the dark to grab you? This part of the ride seems easy. Put your bike in medium gear, take it easy, and I'll show you how to scare those goblins away."

Abby shifted gears. Bill was right. She didn't have to work so hard pedaling in order to keep up the pace he was setting.

"Now, repeat after me," Bill said. Straightening up on his bike, he threw his head back and sang in a strong if somewhat off-key baritone, "Down by the old mill stream/Where I first met you . . ."

Abby laughed. She couldn't help herself—Bill was always doing the unexpected. It seemed crazy to be riding along a darkened highway in the hours just before dawn and singing, but it was just crazy enough to be appealing. Exactly like Bill himself, Abby thought, crazy but appealing.

"Come on, Abby, sing with me," Bill pleaded. "Lift your voice . . . We're doing what we know is fun for us!" He raised his arm in a gesture that was one both of defiance and triumph. "The spooks of darkness take anyone who tries to stop us!" Then, as if seized by some giant bolt of energy, Bill suddenly put his head down, pedaled furiously, and sprinted out in front of Abby. His high spirits were infectious. Abby threw her head back and started to sing the rest of the song, "With your eyes, so blue, dressed in gingham, too . . ." All doubts about the wisdom of what she was doing disappeared.

Singing one old song after another, Bill and Abby rode along, feeling brave, free, and adventurous.

The singing stopped, however, when the asphalt road began its ascent toward the top of Ram's Head

Mountain. It was a gradual climb, but both Abby and Bill had to bend to the task of making their bikes keep up the steady pace they had set.

A few clouds materialized over the face of the moon. The road grew darker, and it was again difficult for Abby to see. She pictured Dale tumbling head over heels from his bike, and she suddenly felt a knot of fear form in her stomach. It was possible that she, too, could have an accident. What would happen if she fell off her bike out here in the dark? Easy, Abby said to herself. You're not a baby. Stop scaring yourself with things that are not going to happen. And anyway, Bill is right here with you.

Remembering how she calmed herself when she became convinced as a child that a terrifying ghost lurked under her bed or in her closet, she began to think of lying on a hot, sunny beach with cool green water lapping at her feet. No ghosts could enter the calm, bright paradise. If she concentrated on that image, Abby knew that even out there on the road she would be able to keep all turbulent thoughts and emotions away.

Bill interrupted her train of thought. "Look!" he said and pointed to a large white sign that gleamed dully at the edge of the road. Abby looked over and read the words, RAM'S HEAD PEAK 3 MILES."

"We're almost there," Bill exclaimed. "We'll be there in plenty of time to catch the first rays. Make you feel good?"

"You bet," Abby answered, trying her best to sound cheerful. She'd be relieved to get off the road, watch the sunrise, then return when the daylight had flooded the highway. The idea of the sun high in the sky was appealing to her.

They continued to pedal along. As if Abby's anxiety had to find an outlet, she realized that she was developing a severe cramp in her left thigh.

Oh, no, not now! Abby thought to herself. I've only got a few more miles left to go. She tried to will the pain away, but with every stroke, it grew worse. Finally, Abby had to call, "Bill, we've got to rest for a minute. I've got a bad leg cramp."

Bill looked back at Abby. Seeing the pain in her face, he quickly pulled to the side of the road. Abby followed, stopped, and dismounted her bike. She sat down in the dewy grass and took her helmet off. She started pounding the outside of her thigh in an effort to make her muscles relax. In her frustration and pain, Abby felt herself very near tears.

Bill came and sat down next to her. "Take it easy, kid," he said. "We've got time."

"It just seems so . . . unfair," Abby said. "Everything seems to be going wrong."

"Nothing is wrong," he said calmly. "You've just got to work this little kink out of your muscles, then we'll be on our way. It's probably the cold that caused it. Here, let me help." Bill reached out and began to massage Abby's thigh. "Doctor Magic Fingers, at your service," he said. "Guaranteed to cure what ails you. As a matter of fact," Bill said as his rubbing became slower and gentler, "I think we ought to make an appointment to do this sometime when you don't have a muscle pull. What do you say?"

Abby pushed his hand away. "I'll think about it, Doctor," she answered, "but this is not the time."

"Well, here's something that might make you change your mind," Bill said. He leaned toward her. Bill gently placed his arm behind Abby's back, guided her toward him, and kissed her.

His movement took Abby by surprise, but as she felt his lips on hers, she couldn't help but respond. She had felt attracted to Bill since she had first seen him, and now he was openly showing his feelings for her. It felt wonderful. Or did it? Despite the excitement that Abby was feeling at Bill's kiss, she suddenly thought what they were doing was—not exactly—but somehow, inappropriate. She hadn't come out on the dark road alone with Bill in order to find a way to make out. No, Abby decided; she had joined him because she really wanted to make it to the top of Ram's Head Mountain. She pulled away from Bill and shook her head.

"What's wrong?" he asked earnestly.

How could she tell him that kisses only served to complicate her feelings about the whole adventure. She was going to have a hard enough time looking Mr. Levin in the eye and telling him the truth about why she left the group. She simply couldn't also add a confession that along the way she and Bill had stopped to kiss. She refused to put herself in a position where she had to lie. Abby thought of herself as an honest person, and as much as she was attracted to Bill, she wasn't going to start being dishonest now. As for Buddy, she wouldn't even think about that until she was back home.

"Bill, I don't think we should," she said, gently pushing him away.

"Why not?" he asked, as he reached out and ran the side of his thumb down her cheek. "I know that you've been wanting to do this since the trip began. I saw you looking at me at the supermarket, around the campfire. Now we can, without Mr. Levin or anyone else interfering."

"Don't be absurd, Bill," Abby said, as she took his hand away from her face. "I certainly wasn't looking at you for the reasons you think. You *are* conceited. It may not make much sense, but I can't go on with this. It's not that I don't find you physically attractive, but something—the situation or the fact that we left the group—I don't know how to explain it, but I can't—that's that."

Bill's voice grew cool and detached. "Sure. I get it. You're a tease. I don't force myself when I'm not wanted. It's so cool. I just thought you might want to add a little spice to our adventure. It seemed a good idea to me. After all, we're both Aries."

"Please don't talk that way, Bill," Abby said. "I'm not a tease. That's an awful thing to say. And I don't want to be 'a little spice' to your adventure. I didn't know you were an Aries, too."

I should have known, Abby thought to herself. Bill's Arian good looks and energy are what attracted me to him, but both being Aries, there's no way our stubborn and headstrong natures can mix.

"Enough," Bill said curtly. The tone of his voice suggested that he was angered by the conversation.

"Besides," said Abby, "judging by the way the

sky is getting lighter over there, it won't be too long until someone will be getting up back at camp. Mr. Levin likes to get up, stir the fire, and get the water boiling. He'll be finding our note. My leg feels better, really it does, so I think we ought to be moving along. Listen, don't be angry. Let's just move on."

"Well, Abby," Bill drawled, "as for Mr. Levin reading your note and rushing up here, I wouldn't give it another thought." He reached into his pocket. "You'll have to think of some other reason not to get involved with me. As you can see, Mr. Levin never got your note." Then, with a smirking grin, he presented it to her with a flourish.

"What's that?" she asked. At first Abby didn't know what Bill was showing her. "What's that?"

"What does it look like?" Bill replied.

"The note to Mr. Levin?" Abby asked. In her own ears her voice sounded like a child's. "But you—"

"No, I didn't," Bill said. "As you can see."

Abby tried to figure out what Bill was trying to do. "You agreed that we'd leave the note," she said. "Why did you do that if you weren't going to leave it?"

"Because, Abby," Bill said as he reached out and took her hand, "I knew I'd never get you to come along if I didn't agree to leave the note. You had that 'frightened deer' look in your eyes, and I wanted you to come with me." He continued quietly, "I didn't want Mr. Levin to know too quickly or too exactly where we had gone. I'm sure he'll figure it out pretty fast, but I thought it would be more of a kick if he had to scurry around a bit. It'd be funnier that way, right?"

In the predawn light Abby looked directly into Bill's face and knew that she didn't like what she saw. She felt disgusted. "'Funnier'?" she asked incredulously. She freed her hand from Bill's grasp. "You think it's funny? It's not funny. It's mean and malicious."

"Oh, come on, Abby, chill out," Bill said. "It's no big deal."

Suddenly, all the things about Bill that Abby had pushed to the back of her mind came rushing forward—his arrogance toward Mr. Levin, his irresponsibility at the supermarket, and the way Bill got out of taking any blame for it. And worse, worse than all of that, was the way Bill had played with her feelings, and the way she had let him. He acted as if he wanted to be a friend and help her reach her goal, but all he wanted was to be a show-off and a big shot. He just wanted to outsmart Mr. Levin, and he had used Abby to do it.

"You know, Bill, I've heard you say that before— 'It's no big deal.' What is a big deal to you? Pulling pranks? What you did in the supermarket with the cart really wasn't funny. It was sadistic. It made the innocent woman hysterical, and it got Dawn into big trouble. She *needs* that job, you know."

"I noticed you were enjoying yourself at the time," Bill said coldly.

"I'm ashamed to say you're right. I was so determined that the trip not be full of losers that I put my hopes in you as a winner. Was I ever wrong!

I thought you weren't a loser, but you're worse. You're a rotten show-off."

"I see. Calling me names, innocent Aries? Sorry that I'm not as entertaining as you would like," Bill answered. "Nonetheless, I'm going to get on my bike and ride to the top of the mountain." He checked his watch. "Sun will be up in about fifteen minutes. After you've come this far, you might as well join me. He looked at Abby directly. "You know, I don't get you. I don't get you at all. I thought you were cool. You seemed sure of yourself. I thought you'd understand, but you don't understand one bit. You're like everybody else." His voice hardened. "Full of that goody-goody teacher's-pet garbage. Don't ever call me a loser again."

"You mean that I don't pull mean tricks, lie, and go out of my way to see how much trouble I can cause?" Abby asked.

"Oh, come off it, Abby!" Bill answered, matching her angry tone with his own. "In case you don't know it, most people are turkeys, and if you can have a little fun with them, why not? No harm done. If they have their turkey feelings hurt a bit, so what? Have a laugh and move on, that's what I say—that's a winner's philosophy."

"Most people are *not* turkeys! If that's the way you feel, you can just get your laughs and move on without me. Better yet, I'm going to move on without you. You know, you've managed to do what no one else could do. You've showed me that getting to the top of Ram's Head this morning is not so important. I'm going back to camp, and I only hope

I can get there before Mr. Levin gets too worried."
Abby realized she was yelling and fighting back tears
of anger. She tried to calm herself. Finally, she said
slowly and calmly, "You can go to the top of the
mountain and get all the laughs you want alone.
Enjoy yourself."

Abby rose from where she was sitting. Her leg
had fallen alseep while she had been resting, but
she was in such a hurry that she paid no attention
to it. She took two steps forward. Before she realized
it, her leg buckled underneath her.

She heard Bill shout, "Abby, wait!" But she
couldn't stop herself from falling and she reached
out her hands to break the fall. She fell awkwardly
and heavily on a jagged rock that jutted out of the
dirt.

Abby heard a dull thud and felt a sharp pain in
her forehead. When she opened her eyes, she saw
that the rock was spotted with dark-colored splotches.
"Oh, no, no, no," she groaned and put her hand to
her head. As she examined her blood-covered palm,
she asked, "What have I done to myself?"

Bill had seen her begin to fall, but had been
powerless to prevent it. He scrambled to his feet.
"Are you okay, Abby?" he asked.

Abby, the blood dripping down her face now,
glared at him.

Bill mumbled as if he were talking to himself.
"This is awful. What do we do? Oh, no."

"Bill," Abby said, as she sat up, "Come over here
and give me something to put on my head. Take a
look and tell me how badly cut I am." She spoke

calmly, trying as best she could not to panic. "Try to see what's happened."

Bill approached and touched Abby's forehead gingerly.

"Ouch! Careful, that hurts."

"I don't know, Abby. Your hair is matted. It looks pretty bad. I . . . I don't feel very well either — blood makes me sick."

"Bill, help me up. Maybe you should ride for help? We've got to do something," Abby said.

"I don't know. Should I leave you? I'm not sure what to do." Bill's voice started to rise to a childlike whine.

Abby began to feel the chill of real fear crawl down her back. She didn't want to panic. She didn't know how badly her head was cut, but she knew the spinning sensation she felt was a bad sign. With Bill in a panic, who was going to be able to help her?

"What am I going to do," she said aloud. Keep calm, keep calm, she reminded herself. Then she slumped backward and fainted.

9

When Abby regained consciousness, she looked up and was surprised to see Mr. Levin. He needed a shave and his face was lined with worry. "Thank goodness," he said.

"Where am I? How did you . . ."

"Take it easy, Abby," said another familiar voice. "Everything is going to be all right." Abby turned her head to the right and saw that Mitchell and Tom were standing over her, too. She read grave concern in Mitch's gray eyes and briefly wondered how badly she was hurt. She closed her eyes for a minute. Was she back at the camp? Had they carried her down the road in some mysterious way? The cold seeping into her back told her she was still where she had fallen.

"You guys are quite a welcoming party," Abby said wanly. "Only I think that I'm the one who should be welcoming you. Where's Bill?"

"I'm here, Abby," she heard Bill answer from somewhere in back of Mr. Levin. She felt so weak that she shut her eyes again. If I just rest a minute, I'll be able to get up, she thought to herself.

Mr. Levin straightened up and turned toward Tom. "She's not in shock. I think she's going to be fine, except for a few stitches to sew up that cut. We'll keep her warm, then we'll take her back down the mountain and get a doctor." He turned to Bill. "As for you," Mr. Levin said, "I don't want to talk about it right now, but I do want you to know that I am very angry with you and that you are in serious, serious trouble."

Bill averted his gaze and mumbled, "Sorry, Mr. Levin. It's just that it seemed like such a kick at the time. We—"

"I'd like to show you a kick," Mr. Levin interrupted, "where it might do you some good. What the devil do you think you were doing? Never mind. I don't think I want to hear the answer."

Abby, vaguely aware of the conversation, opened her eyes and said, "Don't blame Bill, Mr. Levin. I . . . I was wrong, too."

Mr. Levin started to say something, but then he stopped and sighed. "Abby, you, Bill, and I will talk about it later. But for now, let's see if we can get you sitting up. Do you think you can manage that?"

"Yes," Abby replied weakly. "I'm all right, really. It's just that there was all this blood, and my head hurts." She went to feel the cut and found that it had been carefully bandaged.

"You may have a mild concussion. I'm sure that you will have a good headache. Here, have a sip of this. It will warm you up and give you a lift."

Abby reached out tentatively and, taking the top of the thermos Mr. Levin held out to her, swallowed a mouthful of the warm, bitter coffee. She felt it enter her stomach and start a warm glow there. Abby took a few more sips as Marilyn, Tom, and Mitchell watched her anxiously.

"Well, I think everything is under control here," Mr. Levin said. "Tom, take over. Marilyn and Mitchell, give him any help he needs. Don't try to move too much, Abby. I'm going back down and tell Tracey, Fannie, and Dale what has happened up here. I'll go into Allenville, round up a van, and make the necessary phone calls. I should be back in two hours."

Mr. Levin walked toward his bike, and when Bill started to join him, he stopped and said in a low but strained voice, "Stay here. Since we first started to plan this trip, you have been more bother and trouble than you're worth. I thought you had some sense underneath that rough exterior. I am so angry with you, I wish I could throw you off the mountain. Now, follow orders."

Bill held up his hands in his familiar gesture of placation. "Sure, Mr. Levin. I'll wait here until you get back. I didn't think you'd get so upset."

"That's right. As usual, you didn't think," Mr. Levin said. Then he turned on his heel, strode to his bike, mounted it, and began pedaling furiously back toward the camp where the others were waiting.

After he left, an uneasy silence descended on the five who remained behind. Finally, Abby mustered a few words. "What a terrific rescue party. Thanks for finding me . . ."

As if Abby's words had broken the spell of silence,

Marilyn blurted out, "This is *so* incredible, you two. You've ruined everyone's time, and you could have been seriously hurt. Abby, what made you do something so stupid? I can understand Bill, but you?"

"Easy, Marilyn, easy," Mitchell said. "That's not going to change the situation."

"Oh, I know, but we were so *worried*." Marilyn looked at Abby with a mixture of concern and anger. Marilyn's face reminded Abby of the way her mother had looked at her when she had run home in the middle of a terrible summer thunderstorm. She had stayed on the beach too late—the lightning had begun to crackle through the sky before she fled. That look of anger mixed with fright and love was one Abby would never forget.

"Abby's not seriously hurt," Tom said, "and we'll let Mr. Levin take care of the discipline."

Marilyn, close to tears, bit her lip and nodded a silent assent.

"You guys sure knew what to do when you got here," Bill said. "She was bleeding so much I thought she was in big trouble. I admit I was nervous, really."

Tom shrugged. "I don't blame you. Head wounds can look scary. They bleed a lot. Luckily they're not usually as bad as they look."

"You bandaged the cut so well and you know all that," Marilyn said. "Is your father a doctor, Tom?"

Tom laughed. "Hardly. My dad manufactures clothing. I'm not sure he knows a vein from a bone. I guess I just remember biology and some of the stuff we were taught in Boy Scouts first aid."

"Wow, saved by a boy scout! Tom can even write

a college essay about this," Bill said, getting back into his tough-guy self.

"You should be very glad to see this particular boy scout," Marilyn said icily to Bill. "Abby might still be bleeding if you had been the only one around."

"Hey, Marilyn," Bill answered. "I was trying to do something. I was trying to get my jacket under Abby when you arrived. You know, so she wouldn't be lying on the cold ground. I was going to do something about her head next. I really was."

Marilyn rolled her eyes and shook her head.

"When did you get here?" Abby asked. "Marilyn, tell me what happened."

"You had only been lying there for a few minutes," said Bill, "when they rode up like the cavalry to the rescue. Man, was I glad to see them!"

"I'm sorry about all of this. I really am," Abby said to Marilyn. "I didn't mean to spoil everyone's time."

"My guess is that you're not as sorry as you're going to be when Mr. Levin gets through with you," Tom warned.

"Oh, he'll be all right," Bill said. "But most of these teachers are more bark than bite. After all, what can he do? Kill us?"

"The thought has probably crossed his mind more than once," Marilyn said, as she sent Bill an icy glare.

"Marilyn, I get the point," Bill said as he threw up his hands. "But let me and Abby cope with it, all right?"

"How did you get here so fast?" Abby asked.

"Well," Mitchell said, "for some reason I got up earlier than the rest—call of nature, I guess. Anyway, I noticed right away that you weren't in your sleeping bag, Bill. At first I thought that you might be up for the same reason I was. But you didn't come back and I didn't see you or hear you out in the woods, so I woke Mr. Levin. At first he thought that I was just being an alarmist. He was sure that you were around somewhere. In fact, he said that you were probably playing another one of your dumb jokes."

"Thanks a lot," Bill said.

"Well, that's what he said. But the time went by, and you were nowhere to be found. Then, as if he didn't want to do it, he checked the girls' lean-to. When he found out you were gone, too, Abby, he got mad."

"He woke us all up," Marilyn continued, "and asked if any of us knew where you might have gone. I mean the answer was kind of obvious. Of course, Tracey had a few comments about where you were and what you were doing."

"I bet," sighed Abby.

"Since Dale basically was all right and didn't need much attention," Mitch continued, "Mr. Levin asked Marilyn, Tom, and me to ride up here with him. Tracey and Fannie were to search the woods nearby, just in case you might have gotten into some trouble there. It seemed unlikely, but it gave them something to do while we were away."

"You know, Abby, you should have at least left a note if you were going to desert the rest of us."

"Oh, Mitchell, I wanted to," Abby began, but Bill interrupted her.

"Yeah, but we were in a hurry, you know? We didn't start out very early, and we didn't have a lot of time to spare."

Abby couldn't bring herself to look at Bill. She didn't know whether to expose him as a liar or not. His shoddy behavior seemed to have rubbed off on her. All the anger she had recently felt for him came flooding back to her. It was *his* fault that everything got spoiled. How dare he lie on top of it?

But she quickly acknowledged to herself that it was her fault, too. It was too easy to take out all her bad feelings on Bill.

Instead of saying anything about the note, she looked at Mitchell and sadly said, "We really loused it up. I don't blame all of you for being angry."

Mitchell looked at her searchingly as if to see whether or not she was sorry. "This log I'm propped on is getting awfully uncomfortable. Could you pull me up?"

Mitchell helped her to her feet, but he warned, "Go easy, Abby. Mr. Levin said not to move around too much. Take it slow, will you?"

"I just want to stretch. I'm sort of stiff and cold from staying still for so long. Will you give me an arm to lean on?"

"Sure," Mitchell answered, and, placing his arm under hers, he walked with her a few yards away from the others.

The pines on the edge of the road formed a natural barricade, but Abby felt the heat of the sun as it rose above them. She looked at her watch. It was eight o'clock. The dawn of the spring solstice had come and gone, and, despite all her plans, she had missed it. She had not only failed to do the one thing that she had vowed to do before she had left home, but she had done something that she was ashamed of and that she would never have imagined she'd do. Suddenly she felt herself crumple up inside. "Oh, Mitchell this is so terrible," she sobbed.

"You're going to be fine, and Bill's right. Mr. Levin will be angry. Your parents will be angry, and some of the other kids will be angry. But they'll all get over it."

Tears clouded Abby's vision as she looked up at him, "I know that," she sniffled, "but I mean . . . oh, I don't know what I mean. I wanted this trip to be *so* good and then I went and ruined everything. I don't know why I listened to Bill. What's wrong with me, anyhow?" She wiped the tears from her eyes with the back of her hand.

Mitchell gave the elbow that he was holding a gentle squeeze. "Don't be too rough on yourself. Remember I said that I knew something about astrology?"

Abby nodded.

"Well, if I remember correctly, your sign tends to get carried away by your enthusiasm, you know."

"Oh, I know, I know," Abby answered, "but my enthusiasm has always turned out to be so right before."

"Well, you were wrong this time. But to tell you the truth, I'm not mad at you that it turned out the way it did."

"But I ruined everybody's time!"

"Everyone's time was pretty much ruined when Dale fell off his bike," Mitch answered. "And can I tell you something else?"

"Yes."

"You're right about one important thing. Bill Kelsey *is* a jerk. I don't know what happened between the two of you. It's none of my business, but I'm glad you've finally seen through him."

Abby glanced back over her shoulder to where Bill, Marilyn, and Tom were sitting. Bill obviously hadn't lost his touch. He was just finishing a story about something and Marilyn, who had been so angry and distant with him only moments ago, threw her head back and laughed.

"If you thought he was a jerk, why didn't you say so to me?"

Mitchell smiled ruefully. "Abby, I guess you haven't noticed, but since the first meeting to organize this trip, I tried to get your attention," he said in a rush. "And when you're, ah, interested in a girl, you don't go up to her and tell her that the guy she seems to be interested in is a loser and you're better." Mitchell looked down at his sneakers. Abby noticed that he was blushing. She stared at him for a few seconds. Then she broke into a delighted giggle.

"You're right, Mitchell. And you know what? You really do remind me of Jimmy Stewart! And that's a compliment."

"Are you talking about the actor, or is he an old boyfriend?" he asked, not sure whether he had heard correctly.

"The actor, not a boyfriend!" Abby laughed.

"Really?" he asked. When he offered her his arm again, she accepted and they smiled at each other.

"Hey Abby, how about joining the other outcast," Bill called. "Or have you deserted me for the scientist or maybe you'll choose the boy scout!" pointing at Tom. "She's a real flirt."

"Enough, Bill," she said to him in a stern voice. "Let's not call each other names or I'll get nasty, too."

Bill put his hands over his head as if to ward off a blow and said, "Ouch!"

"As for Tom," Abby said, "he may have been a boy scout, but I'm awfully glad he was. He helped me when you were in a panic."

"And what do you have to say, Mr. Florence Nightingale?" Bill said fliply to Tom.

"Kelsey," Tom replied, "you may think you are funny, but you're not. I have three well-chosen words for you . . ."

"This threatens to become an argument," Marilyn interrupted. "I'm awfully tired of bickering and fighting. Anyone want to have a light conversation about nuclear war, or would you prefer to play Telephone?"

Her words effectively broke the tension in the situation. The five of them managed to pass the next hour without fighting. Abby sat quietly. The bandage on her head seemed to have stopped the bleeding, but the pounding across her forehead and nose did not disappear.

Finally Tom said, "Wait a minute. I hear something."

They all listened. Sure enough, the sound of a

motor came closer and closer. Before long, a pickup roared up the road toward them.

"Rescued at last," Marilyn said as she broke into a large grin.

As the truck drew up beside them, Abby read PHILLIPS' LUMBER, ALLENVILLE on the side of the cab. She could see that all the other kids, as well as their bikes, were in the truck's flat bed.

Mr. Levin rolled down the window of the cab and said, "Ride up here with me, Abby. Help her in, boys."

Tracey looked down at Abby and said with a grimace, "Well, well, our romantic runaways, found at long last. Thank you, Bill. Thank you, Abby, for putting the finishing touch on a really grand experience. Now I will have the privilege of arriving home early. My parents will be *so* pleased. But of course, yours will really be amused."

Abby hung her head and opened the door opposite Mr. Levin. There was nothing to say. Tracey was mean, but she was right.

As Mitchell hoisted his bike and then Abby's aboard the truck, he called, "Hey, Tracey, give her a break, will you."

"Thank you," Abby mouthed quietly to herself and she stepped up into the cab.

They waited while the other bikes were put on the truck and secured. Bill, Tom, Mitch, and Marilyn climbed aboard, Mr. Levin turned the key, and the engine roared to life.

"Well, that ends that," Mr. Levin said as he made a U-turn and headed back to town.

Mr. Levin didn't say another word as he drove

along. Abby found herself gazing out the window watching the scenery slip by. The bright sun hit the landscape, creating patches of shadows. If she had not been so upset, Abby would have relished the beauty of the spring day.

Finally, Mr. Levin broke the silence. "If it had been Fannie or even Tracey who got involved with Bill, I might not be surprised. You seemed too bright. I don't understand."

The words stung. Abby, who had been wondering the same thing herself, replied, "I don't either, Mr. Levin. I think that maybe I didn't listen to the better part of myself. I had so many expectations and something to prove to myself and my friends, I got carried away. It's part of my Aries personality."

"Please, don't blame the stars for your behavior," Mr. Levin said in an aggravated tone.

"I'm not doing that," Abby answered. "It's just that most of my Zodiac Club friends were going to a party this weekend. I decided against going even though they thought I was silly to do so."

"Why didn't you go with them?" Mr. Levin asked.

"I might have, but I had signed up for your trip, and I'm stubborn, I guess. I just couldn't change my mind. I came on this trip determined that I was going to have just as good a time as the Zodiacs. I wanted to be on top of Ram's Head just as I told them I would."

Mr. Levin said with a sigh, "You picked the wrong person to help you achieve your goal. Bill has been disruptive in my classes. I almost didn't allow him to come on this trip, but I thought maybe he'd chosen to come because he loved the outdoors and would, therefore, behave."

Abby glanced over and saw the muscles in Mr. Levin's jaw tighten as he cut himself off from saying anything more about Bill Kelsey.

"Oh, Mr. Levin," Abby said, "I can't say anything except that you're right and I'm sorry. I am really sorry."

Mr. Levin kept his eyes on the road as he replied, "I know you are sorry, Abby, but there are some things that 'I'm sorry' can't fix. Your punishment, as far as I'm concerned, comes from losing my trust and that of the other people on the trip. What your parents say and do when you arrive home early is up to them." He smiled ruefully. "I guess you'll have plenty to tell that club of yours. I can't believe that your girlfriends wouldn't have understood if weather and an accident kept you from your goal."

Abby nodded and thought about the other members of the Zodiac Club. None of them would have made fun of her for not making it to the top of Ram's Head because of Dale's accident — they would have been sympathetic. She was the one who wanted to do it for herself. But now, would any of them understand why she did what she did? She hoped they'd try.

10

They drove into Allenville where Mr. Levin had arranged for Abby to see the local doctor. Abby protested that she was all right, but Mr. Levin insisted. Mr. Levin pulled the truck into the parking lot of the small brick medical building. The kids in the back climbed out, eager to stretch and find a place to buy soft drinks. Dale wanted to know why Abby was getting all the attention when he was injured too. Mr. Levin assured him that the doctor was willing to look at his ankle. So Dale joined them as Abby and Mr. Levin entered Dr. Harvey's office.

The large waiting room was filled with wiggling kids and their patient mothers trying to keep them under control. Dale and Abby were able to find seats together. Mr. Levin asked the receptionist if he could use the phone while they waited.

"What really went on with you and Kelsey up there?" asked Dale, eager for the opportunity to question her alone.

"What do you mean?" Abby responded. "You know the story."

"Yeah, I know what you two said to Mr. Levin. But what's the *real* story. Everybody at school knows what kind of a guy Bill Kelsey is. He didn't take off with you in the middle of the night because of his love of sunrises. Be serious, Abby."

Abby didn't know what to say. Dale expected to hear some juicy gossip. She stared at the impatient expression on his face.

"But what I said was true, at least for me," responded Abby rather feebly. She couldn't deny, however, that the story sounded fishy, even to her.

"Well," Dale continued, as if he were talking about a soap, "Tracey says that you've been coming on to Kelsey since the trip started . . ."

"Tracey," Abby exploded, her voice rising above the din created by the children in the room. "Leave it to me to make a mistake when the viper is along. She'd better not spread this story all over Collingwood. She'll probably have me spending the night alone in the woods with him."

Abby's voice cracked and her anger turned to tears. Dale watched her eyes fill as Mr. Levin crossed the room.

Abby and Mr. Levin were ushered into the doctor's office. Mr. Levin recapped the incident for the doctor. "Had a nasty fall, hmmm?" he asked as he gently removed the bandage that Tom had put on her head. "It's a pretty bad cut," he continued as he reached for some disinfectant, "but I don't think it will require stitches. Whoever did this butterfly bandage knew what he was doing. Now hold on, this might sting."

He placed new bandages on her forehead and then shone a light in her eye. "Look here, please," he asked. He examined her closely and announced that there seemed to be no concussion. "You'll be fine in a few days, nothing but a small scar to show for the accident." Turning to Mr. Levin, he said, "Just make sure she's watched for signs of drowsiness, blurred vision, or dizziness for the next forty-eight hours."

Great, Abby thought. That's all I need—a scar to add to the list of this week's disasters.

"How's your head?" Dale asked as Abby came out.

"I'm fine," Abby was barely able to whisper a reply. She told Mr. Levin that she would wait in the truck while the doctor took care of Dale. Abby climbed into the empty cab, put her head against the dashboard, and sobbed. All she could think of was the field day Tracey would have spreading her version of the bike trip all over school. Everyone would be talking about her running off with Bill Kelsey. Kids love gossip. All of her friends, her parents, the teachers—everyone would hear it. Would they believe it?

She heard the cab door open, and Mr. Levin got in. He put his hand on her shoulder. "Are you all right, Abby?" he asked. She nodded yes but did not look at him. The other kids climbed on the back. Mr. Levin reached out and started the engine. The cab was quiet except for the sounds of Abby's sobbing.

* * *

"Well, here we are," said Mr. Levin as he pulled the truck into the Martins' driveway. "Your parents are expecting you. I phoned them and the other parents from Dr. Harvey's office." Mr. Levin walked her down the drive while Mitchell and Tom brought her gear and her bike from the truck. Abby barely set foot on the driveway when her mother ran out to meet her.

"Abby, Abby," she cried, "are you all right? Oh, look at your head!" Abby felt the warm arms of her mother envelop her in a hug.

"Mom, I'm so sorry, I . . ." And the tears came again.

Abby saw her father approaching with a troubled frown on his face.

"Oh, Dad, I meant for this to be a great trip," she sobbed.

"We'll talk about it inside," Mr. Martin said, wrapping his arm around her shoulder. "Mr. Levin, I'm sure that we need to have a talk, but for now, we'd like to get Abby inside and to bed. We appreciate your care and concern and we apologize for the trouble Abby's caused."

Abby's head pounded, more from the humiliation of hearing her father apologize than from the pain of her sore forehead. And he didn't even know that the other kids were talking about her and Bill. How would she face her parents when that story got to them? She knew Tracey would make certain it got around. All Abby wanted to do was to get to her room, close the door, and escape from all this. But she managed to thank Mr. Levin and wave a meager goodbye to the others.

11

The shrill ring of the phone next to her bed jarred Abby from her sound sleep.

"Hello," she muttered drowsily.

A cheery voice responded, "Abby, hi, just called to check up on you. How's your head?"

The voice sounded unfamiliar to the half-awake Abby. "Who is this?" she asked.

"It's me, Marilyn. I guess I woke you. How are you feeling?"

Abby realized that it was the Marilyn, Marilyn from the trip.

"Marilyn, I can't believe you're calling. I didn't think any one of you would want to talk to me after the way I messed things up."

"Well, I can't speak for all the others, but I don't feel that way. Remember, Dale's accident came first."

"Yes, that's true," replied Abby. "But he didn't disgrace himself the way I did."

"What do you mean?" Marilyn asked. "So you did a dumb thing—but everyone's human."

"No, no, not that," Abby replied. "Dale told me what everyone thinks—I mean that it was just an excuse for me to be alone and make out with Bill."

"Do you mean Tracey?"

"Well, Dale told me what she had been saying when we were waiting in the doctor's office. The thought of facing the kids in school is five times more painful than the lump on my head."

"Look, Abby," Marilyn said kindly, "I'm not going to tell you that no one will talk about this. People love a juicy story. But your real friends will know it's not true. And I don't think that Fannie and Tom and the others will support that gossip. While we were waiting outside the doctor's office, we all talked about stupid situations we had gotten into."

"I hope you're right, Marilyn," replied Abby, "but it will be horrible enough to face my own parents and explain it all to them, let alone the entire cafeteria at Collingwood High. I don't know how I'm going to do that. You're terrific to have called. Just knowing that you're talking to me makes me feel a little better. Thanks, Marilyn."

Abby hung up the phone and tried to drift off to sleep again. Thoughts of her parents' reactions and those of her girlfriends went around and around in her head, until she fell into a restless sleep.

Abby slept through to the next morning. She wasn't even aware of the several times her mother or father had come in during the night and given her a little shake to make sure that she was conscious and not suffering the results of a concussion. She had been totally exhausted.

Breakfast the next morning was hard to face. Abby's feelings of humiliation, her poor judgment about Bill Kelsey, and everything else tumbled out. The look of disappointment on her parents' faces was almost punishment enough, although Abby knew she might not remember thinking that during the month she was going to be grounded. As their discussion ended, Cathy Rosen appeared at the back door.

"Cathy, how come you're not still at Penny's, and how did you know I'm home?" Abby asked.

"Slow up, one thing at a time, Ab. Number one, I ran into Tracey Kingsport at the diner last night. She couldn't wait to tell me how my good Aries friend from the Zodiac Club had made a disaster out of Mr. Levin's bike trip and her last high-school spring vacation."

"Oh, boy. I can imagine what she was saying about me." Abby sighed.

"Well, short of starting a world war, you seem to be responsible for everything else. I can see that she was right about your hitting your head, but was she right about you and Bill Kelsey? What happened with him?"

"Oh, Cathy. I acted like a jerk—and am I going to pay for it!"

"What do you mean?" Cathy asked with a questioning expression on her face. "Did you really go off with him alone one night? What about Buddy?"

"Oh don't start, please. Well, yes and no." Abby's eyes filled with tears. She dreaded the thought of telling Cathy about how stupid she had been. "I didn't think. When Dale Chambers, you know, the overweight one, turned his ankle, it was doubtful that we were going to get to Ram's Head for the morning of the equinox. You know how much I was counting on that. Well, Bill Kelsey had been paying a lot of attention to me all during the trip. He can be really cool when he tries, and I kind of liked his attention. I didn't even get to tell you that Buddy called right before the trip and at the last minute invited me to visit. Then, when I said I couldn't, he said maybe some other time, but didn't make a definite date. He hung up and I felt bad. So when everything was coming apart on the trip, and Bill suggested we leave early to go to the top of Ram's Head to see the sunrise without the group, I figured I would. I don't know where my brain was. I never expected anything to happen. I asked him to leave a note I wrote for Mr. Levin, but he didn't." Abby's words began to race, she began to sob. "Oh, Cathy. We only left two hours before daybreak. I wasn't in the woods with him all night. When I fell, he just came apart—all his big talk was gone. If the others hadn't followed us, I don't know what would have . . ."

Shaking her head, Cathy interrupted. "I can't believe you just up and left a teacher like that. It's not like you, Abby. And with Bill Kelsey. Mara told you that stuff he pulled last year. Did you forget?"

"I just don't know. I did learn one thing on this trip, besides the fact that two Aries are no match. I realize that I've been too hard on people. I've dismissed nice guys like Tom and Mitchell without getting to know them at all. I assumed they were losers just because they were different from boys like Buddy or Will. It's a hard way to learn a lesson.

Now, I don't know what they think of me. And look at this," Abby moaned, as she pulled her hair off her forehead. "A nice scar to top it all off."

"Oh, Abby, it's hardly noticeable," Cathy assured her.

"But it's there for good. I'll have to come up with some way to hide it."

"Well, why don't you stop thinking about your troubles long enough to ask me why I'm home from Penny's in the middle of the holiday?" Cathy asked, trying to lighten Abby's mood.

"I forgot all about it. What happened?" Abby asked.

"Well, you know Murphy's Law—everything that can go wrong, will. It was in full operation at the Rosses' this weekend. First, we got a flat tire on the way to the lake. The trunk of the car was totally stuffed with all our duffels and bags of food for the weekend and we had to empty it all over the road to get to the spare tire. Mr. Ross changed the tire, grumping the whole time, and then we tried to fit all the stuff back in the trunk and it just wouldn't go. It took us forever to get there."

Abby began to smile as Cathy continued, "And you know that astrology expert. Well, he was good-looking and he was over thirty, but not by much. And he brought his very pregnant wife and two-year-old kid with him. The kid was cute, but it was not the romantic situation we had in mind. And Mr. Ross made a little mistake about his expertise in astrology, a two-letter mistake, like an *l* and a *g*. The guy was really into astronomy, not astrology.

He brought this huge telescope with him and he lectured on the positions of the planets and the constellations! All we wanted to do at that point was go in and watch TV. Penny was crazed."

Abby began to giggle. She could just imagine everyone's reaction!

"The second night was rainy and overcast. Anyway we were still having fun, though not as planned, when the furnace shut off. After about twelve hours, it got really cold and damp in the house. The Rosses couldn't get a repairman on the weekend, so we took that as our final omen and packed up and came home. At least no flat tires this time. Some weekend, huh.

The only way we could salvage any of it was Saturday night, before the furnace broke down, we looked up famous people who were born under our signs in some book that Jessica brought along. As a matter of fact, I made a copy of the list. I figured you'd want to see it."

"Thanks." Abby took the list that Cathy had pulled from her bag. Of course, she turned to Aries first, but she was curious about all the signs.

ARIES

Desi Arnaz	Robert Frost	Gregory Peck
Warren Beatty	Vincent van Gogh	Diana Ross
Marlon Brando	Harry Houdini	Spencer Tracy
Joan Crawford	Thomas Jefferson	Tennessee
Aretha Franklin	Scarlett O'Hara	Williams

TAURUS

Fred Astaire	Queen Elizabeth II	Karl Marx
Charlotte Brontë	Sigmund Freud	Ricky Nelson
Archie Bunker	Adolf Hitler	William
Carol Burnett	Audrey Hepburn	Shakespeare
Cher	Shirley MacLaine	Barbara Streisand

GEMINI

Joan Collins	Lillian Hellman	Paul McCartney
Bob Dylan	Bob Hope	Joe Namath
Sarah Fabiny	John F. Kennedy	Vincent Price
Ian Fleming	Henry Kissinger	Queen Victoria
Judy Garland	Stan Laurel	Walt Whitman

CANCER

John Q. Adams	Princess Diana	George Orwell
Milton Berle	John Glenn	Linda Ronstadt
James Cagney	Ernest Hemingway	Ringo Starr
Captain	Lena Horne	Henry David
Kangaroo	Helen Keller	Thoreau

LEO

Lucille Ball	Alfred Hitchcock	Robert Redford
Emily Brontë	Aldous Huxley	Yves Saint-
Fidel Castro	Gene Kelly	Laurent
Amelia Earhart	Napoleon	Andy Warhol
Valerie Harper	Jacqueline Onassis	Mae West

VIRGO

Anne Bancroft	Greta Garbo	Mickey Mouse
Lauren Bacall	Michael Jackson	O. Henry
Leonard Bernstein	D. H. Lawrence	Peter Sellers
Peter Falk	Sophia Loren	Twiggy
Elliott Gould	Grandma Moses	Leo Tolstoy

LIBRA

Julie Andrews	Johnny Carson	Gandhi
Art Buckwald	Jimmy Carter	John Lennon
Sarah Bernhardt	Dwight Eisenhower	Groucho Marx
Brigitte Bardot	F. Scott Fitzgerald	Walter Matthau
Truman Capote	George Gershwin	Barbara Walters

SCORPIO

Marie Antoinette	Marie Curie	Goldie Hawn
Richard Burton	Count Dracula	Katharine
Walter Cronkite	Richard Dreyfuss	Hepburn
Prince Charles	Art Garfunkel	Mahalia Jackson
		Robert Kennedy

SAGITTARIUS

Beethoven	Donald Duck	Eleanor Roosevelt
Walt Disney	Jane Fonda	Charles Schultz
Joe DiMaggio	Mary Martin	Frank Sinatra
Kirk Douglas	Harpo Marx	Dionne Warwicke

CAPRICORN

Muhammad Ali   Cary Grant   Ethel Merman
Clara Barton   Diane Keaton   Richard Nixon
George Burns   Martin Luther   Elvis Presley
Al Capone   King, Jr.   Edgar Allan Poe
Marlene Dietrich   Rudyard Kipling   Jane Wyman

AQUARIUS

Jack Benny   Clark Gable   Paul Newman
Lewis Carroll   James Joyce   Yoko Ono
James Dean   Abraham Lincoln   Ronald Reagan
Charles Darwin   Charles Lindbergh   Burt Reynolds
Mia Farrow   Wolfgang Mozart   John Travolta

PISCES

Harry Belafonte   George Harrison   Sidney Poitier
Elizabeth Barrett   Ted Kennedy   Auguste Renoir
    Browning   Jerry Lewis   Elizabeth Taylor
Fréderic Chopin   Michelangelo   George
Albert Einstein   Liza Minnelli   Washington

"You forgot Mick Jagger," Abby said.

"Why are you still in love with him?" Cathy asked. "The Stones aren't even that hot anymore. Anyway, this weekend was such a fiasco, you're lucky I remembered to bring you anything."

Cathy could certainly tell a story when she got started. Abby was feeling better just from being with her. The rest of the day brought more surprises—phone calls from the Zodiacs and kids on the trip to see how she was. Even Tracey called. Abby couldn't believe it.

Late in the afternoon, just as she was thinking about a nap, the doorbell rang. "I'll get it," Abby said. She felt well enough to walk around the house and was eager for company.

She opened the door and gave a gasp of pleasure. There stood Mitchell, holding a beautiful bouquet of spring flowers.

"Hi," he said. "These are for you."

"For me?" Abby asked.

"Yes," Mitchell replied. "If I'm not mistaken, they're very much like the ones Jimmy Stewart used to give to his female lead in the movies."

Abby smiled. "That's so nice," she said.

"Abby, I have something to tell you," Mitchell said, trying to be serious. "After we got home yesterday, I went down to the library and looked up our signs in one of the astrology books. As you know, I am an Aquarius. Interesting, right? And do you know what one of the few signs compatible with the headstrong, exciting Aries woman is?" He gave her a wink. "The air sign Aquarius. Since Aries is a fire sign, and air causes fire to burn more brightly, we're a match with great potential."

Abby smelled the bouquet and then gave a laugh of pleasure. "I don't know, Mitchell, after the last few days, I've decided not to rely on the stars as much as on my own brains and intuition."

"Hey, you're not going to give up on the stars when we're a team made in heaven?" he answered.

"No," she replied. "I'm still a staunch member of the Zodiac Club."

"Are you feeling up for a walk?" he asked.

"I'd love to," Abby said. "Just wait a minute until I put these flowers in water and get a jacket."

She ran back to the kitchen, grabbed a sweater, and quickly put the flowers in a vase. Before her mother had a chance to stop her, Abby ran down the hall to where Mitchell was waiting.

"Let's go," she said. "It's spring outside, my favorite time of year."

Join in the fun when THE ZODIAC CLUB™ meets again in the following books:

THE STARS UNITE
(21106-3)
When summer doldrums hit, Abby Martin and her friends decide to change their fortunes by forming a club based on Abby's new passion, astrology. Little do they realize what the stars hold in store!

ARIES RISING
(21107-1)
What could be more perfect for Abby, an Aries, than a bike trip to Ram's Head Mountain at the spring equinox? Joining her science class on the trip means passing up a Zodiac Club weekend party, but Abby is ready for some adventure of her own...

TAURUS TROUBLE
(21109-8)
When Danny Burns scoops Cathy Rosen's story during their internship at the local newspaper, Cathy, a Leo, is roaring mad. Can she grab the bull by the horns and put the arrogant Taurus in his place?

LIBRA'S DILEMMA
(21108-X)
When Mara's boyfriend, Doug, is involved in a cheating scandal at Collingwood High, it's hard for Mara, the perfect Libra, to remain an impartial judge. Should she defend the guy she loves—or the principles she lives by?

$1.95 each

BOOKS FOR YOUNG ADULTS

Available at your local bookstore or library.

Join THE ZODIAC CLUB

You can be part of THE ZODIAC CLUB.
Share the fun and adventures
with the founding members.

Just fill out and return the coupon below
and you will receive:

★ **membership card** ★
★ **free personalized computerized horoscope** ★
★ **upcoming news of Zodiac Club titles** ★
★ **and more surprises** ★

_____ Yes! Enroll me in THE ZODIAC CLUB

Please send me my free personalized
computerized horoscope.

Name _____ Age _____

Address _____

City/State _____ Zip _____

Birthdate _____
          Day   Month   Year

                     A.M.
Time of birth _____ P.M. Place of birth _____
                                        City   State

Please enclose $1.50 to cover postage and handling.
Send check or money order — no cash or C.O.D.'s
please.

MAIL TO: Box Zodiac 2
                Pacer Books
                The Putnam Publishing Group
                51 Madison Avenue
                New York, NY 10010